Apni Zaban:

Invisible and Unscripted

Poetry and Prose in Pahari-Pothwari
with English translation

©2025 Nabeela Ahmed. Each of the literary works in this publication is produced with the permission of its authors.

The right of Nabeela Ahmed to be identified as the editor of this work and the author of the introduction has been asserted by her in accordance with the Copyright, Design and Patents Act 1988.

All rights reserved. No parts of this publication may be reproduced, stored, in a retrieval system, or transmitted, in any form, or by any means, (electronic, mechanical, photocopying, recording or otherwise) without the prior written permission of the publisher.

An Anthology by

The Pahari-Pothwari Literature Project

Compiled and Edited by

Nabeela Ahmed |2025

Funded by

City of Culture Bradford 2025

Contents

Introduction ~ Nabeela Ahmed　　1
Acknowledgements　　6
Participants List　　8

LANGUAGE
My Pahari • Abdul Karim　　10
Boli • Awais Hussain　　12
Zaban Apni • *Nafeesa Hamid*　　15
Zubaan • *Nafisa Akhtar*　　19

Dreams • *Imran Hafeez*　　21
Tongue • *Nabeela Ahmed*　　23
Mari Zaban • *Farah Nazir*　　25

THIRD SPACE
Sarah Shehr Birmingham • *Nafeesa Hamid*　　30
Pakistan naa Sair • *Kausar Mukhtar*　　34
Pehchan • *Awais Hussain*　　35
Sharminda • *Imran Hafeez*　　39
Foreign Living • *Abdul Karim*　　41
A Place In-between • *Nabeela Ahmed*　　44
Tyrah Saal • *Kausar Mukhtar*　　48

NATURE
Maari Sehli • *Nafisa Akhtar*	51
At h pehr • *Awais Hussain*	54
Green Bradford • *Nabeela Ahmed*	58
Son of an Owl • *Abdul Karim*	60
Bradford's Beauty • *Nafisa Akhtar*	63

Lajj • Iftikhar Kalwal   64

SIN
Girls a Sin • *Nabeela Ahmed*	79
Sin • *Abdul Karim*	84
Humans Playing God • *Kausaar Mukhhtar*	86
Ammi Nay Rahm Vich • *Farah Nazir*	87
Gunah • *Awais Hussain*	93
Sazaa • *Nafisa Akhtar*	97

LOVE LETTERS TO OUR PAST AND FUTURE
Abba Ji • *Nafisa Akhtar*	100
A Letter for My Elders and Youngsters • *Nabeela Ahmed*	104
What You Can Get in Our Village •Nafeesa Hamid	108

ROMANTIC LOVE

Eh din nava Nakor • *Imran Hafeez* — 111
Love Language • *Nabeela Ahmed* — 114
Jori ni Jor • *Farah Nazir* — 118
Pyar ka Mausam • *Kausar Mukhta* — 125
Pyar aur Waqt • *Kausar Mukhtar* — 126
I Had Gone to Search for a Poem • *Abdul Raouf Qureshi* — 127
A loose translation of Sonnet 18 in Pahari-Pothwari • *Awais Hussain* — 136
A Wedding at Home in Birmingham • Nafeesa Hamid — 138
Mey Pyaar Kitha Si • *Nafisa Akhtar* — 145

Lucy • Abdul Raouf Qureshi — 149

Introduction

For twenty-eight years, I have had the privilege of teaching a range of subjects from Speech Therapy, and Family Learning, to Creative Writing and Multilingual Poetry to people ranging from reception-aged children to pensioners in Bradford and all over Britain. Whenever the subject of my language, or the Asian or Muslim elements of our identity arose, people often complained of the limited literature available about these ideas.

Teachers would often point out to me (with a subtle request to do something about it!) that they did not have material that was relatable to so many children of Pakistani/Kashmiri heritage and never anything in their mother tongue.

During my creative writing workshops, I saw the excitement and engagement of children once they could include words from the languages and dialects they spoke and noted how they listened in pin drop silence when I shared a poem with them in Pahari-Pothwari. They often giggled as they have never heard their mother tongue used in a formal setting; this would often be followed by them sharing how glad they were to hear it and how much they understood. Teachers are forever telling me that students never engage with poetry like they do in my sessions.

Adult acquaintances are curious to see our lives reflected in literature, and those from my own background could not find the material to read that had representation, using words how they blend multiple languages, and never anything in Pahari-Pothwari in a bookshop or a library.

Pahari-Pothwari is an invisible language spoken by around 70% of the British Pakistani diaspora. Just like languages such as Gaelic and Doric that have suffered fates leaving them without any use in formal settings, Pahari-Pothwari has suffered an even greater injury whereby even most of it's native speakers will refer to it using names such as Punjabi, Mirpuri or simply apni zaban (meaning 'my language'). This has had huge implications for the confidence of the speakers, for access to services and has limited people feeling able to engage in arts and cultural activities in Britain.

For many years I have wanted to respond to this gap and need by creating new literature. City of Culture Bradford 2025 accepted my application for an Artist Award and thus this project began.

With this project I wanted to work with adults and children to create two bodies of work that are rooted in Britain, have translations in English so it is accessible to everyone, and the participants can use whichever script they are comfortable with, whether that is the Persio-Arabic script or the transliteration using the Roman script.

For adults, I did a community call out and selected most writers from Bradford. I held six online sessions asking the group to select themes they wished to write about.

After I contacted several schools, Carlton Bolling and St Bede's and St Joseph's College responded positively. I facilitated six creative writing sessions based on themes they saw as relevant to them from identity, to hobbies, festivals and the unexpected topic of grief; this came up for a few children, and so their powerful poems have been included, often using pseudonyms they chose as they found them too personal to share with their own names on. Two children from Carlton Keighley where I delivered a creative writing course this year had incorporated so much of Pahari-Pothwari language and culture into their work, that I invited them to be a part of this anthology and the showcase.

Creating anthologies has plenty of challenges, but creating one based on a language that does not have a dictionary, or a fixed set of spellings, where participants have a wide range of abilities in speaking their mother tongue, from being fluent, to only speaking about 50% of it, and where it contains multiple ways of pronouncing the same word presented this project with more challenges than I had anticipated!

One challenge not mentioned above is confidence. For the adults it brought forth an inner struggle. The unfamiliarity of thinking for writing in Pahari-Pothwari about a topic that they usually used English or Urdu for posed a real internal battle before they were able to get past the point where it was possible.

The result are two books.

The children focussed on poetry with a different theme each week. You get to see what is important to 13–14-year-olds living in Bradford in 2025. They are proud of their skin colour, their faith and very sure that their British side must be included and visible. They compared the various labels they carry, wrote about sports from boxing to football, and their hobbies of watching Japanese and Korean films comparing the plots with British and Indian films they watch and wrote of how their favourite day was the monthly day out to bowling, and Nandos. They worried about world affairs, and about boxes on every form calling them British, but insisting they tick Bengali or Pakistani and in their poetry, they question: what does it all really mean? They all had celebrations they loved from Bonfire night, to their birthday rituals and one child wrote a vivid piece describing how, when he grows up, he will become a farmer in Kashmir—capturing every detail with care. His words echoed the dreams of a generation he never knew, yet somehow carries within him.

The adults wrote their first letter, in their own language, to fathers who are no longer here and talked and had a go at writing a love poem, which having never read one and reflecting on the modest behaviour expected of no overt expressions of romantic love in the community, came harder than one would expect. You have a Pahari-Pothwari translation of Shakespeare's Sonnet 18. The topic of sin brought out the fury at patriarchy and how different religions portray it. Nature and love combined to produce one of the most lyrical poems full of imagery of birds, trees and plants you will ever read. Two of the adults are beginner writers of short stories and created one each for this anthology. *Lajj* looks at the subject of bringing a spouse over from Pakistan, even when the person from Britain is not a suitable match, the power of the British passport and honour. Lucy looks at how Pakistani men form relationships with white women, without much thought of religion, have children and then once they choose to focus on that side, they consider everything they have as haram and walk away and the consequences of that for the women and children.

This is an anthology of work in Pahari and Pothwari. However, it is written in Bradford, a multicultural space. Pahari-Pothwari is an invisible language. The teachers could not check in the records and see which child speaks Pahari-Pothwari and invite them to the session. They used their judgement and managed to identify the children who said they spoke Punjabi or Mirpuri at home and they were right. In one school, we could not separate two friends: one whose mother tongue was Pashto and despite it being explained that this project is focussed on Pahari-Pothwari, he appeared each week, sat down and wrote a poem in Pashto and English. They have been proof-read by a Bradfordian academic who speaks Pashto and are included too. From the other school, we have a young writer who spoke Urdu and Bengali and insisted he wanted to stay, so his work in Bengali has been proof read by a Bradfordian Bengali poet. I want there to be a space in Britain where speakers of different languages can have opportunities to read and write in those languages and so I felt it was necessary to begin this space here with this anthology.

As there is no fixed way of spelling a word, and within a local area words are pronounced slightly differently to the next area, when editing and proof reading, we have been mindful to keep those differences. This is step one of the journey of writing in Pahari-Pothwari in Britain. Some people spelt teh, others te for and. Some wrote Ek, others ik or ikh for one. Some people added dots and dashes to the top and bottom of letters, others used a capital N at the end of a word to cover that short quick echo of the n sound in a word, that is not pronounced clearly, but exists.

I kept the whole range. It demonstrates where we are at. There is a lot of work to do, a dictionary with common spellings, letters in the Persio-Arabic script that do not exist in Urdu, Arabic, Persian or Punjabi. Continuous new material for people to read in both scripts alongside the opportunities to write and critique this work to develope people's confidence in reading and writing in Pahari-Pothwari. I see it as the first step on a ladder, with a long way to go before you reach the first floor. This is fine. There is a Chinese proverb that says, once you have taken the first step, you are half way there.

Acknowledgements

I am grateful for City of Culture Bradford 2025 for granting me *The Artist's Award*, which has enabled me to deliver these two anthologies and showcase this work.

Teachers in every school have a tremendous workload, so to take on an extra project is not an easy task. I am indebted to Vinita Mahmood from Carlton Bolling who said, 'Our children need this opportunity.' And to Farhat Alam who had just taken up a new post at the school and despite this said, 'Yes, this is an invaluable experience and such a rare opportunity. I don't want my school to miss out.'

They both made the time to organise the sessions, the children, gathered their work, shared it with me and both did not just select the children who are picked for all the opportunities, but included those with additional needs who we supported during each session. Some of the richest poems were written by these children.

Without both of their support this project could not have happened.

Justine Manning is the librarian at Carlton Keighley who worked closely with the children from the creative writing group and has supported the two children to be a part of this anthology and the showcase event.

Dr Mediah Ahmed proofread the children's work after me and reassured me that it will make sense to the readers. Mr Ahsan Ullah proofread the work in Bengali and agreed to share one of his poems in both languages on stage alongside Sahir Ahmed, so he is not the only person who is sharing in Bengali on the night. I am grateful for his kindness. Dr Amir Khan, proofread Ziyad Khan's work in Pashto. Thank you for all your support.

I'd like to thank children who took a leap of faith and had a go, even though they had no reference of how to do this and gave it their best.

All the adult participants found time from their busy schedules to have a go at something they were not sure about, most had never tried anything like this before and found unexpected internal and external challenges in writing in Pahari-Pothwari, and in writing poetry. I am grateful for the trust you placed in me and for your support and encouragement along the way.

I am grateful to the team at City of Culture, Bradford 2025 who have supported me with marketing, events management, press and everything related to enabling a showcase the participants and project deserved.

Finally, a big thank you to my family who keep asking which book I am talking about, and which book I am currently editing- you are, as always, the backbone of all my events.

Participants

Dr Farah Nazir

Imran Hafeez

Kausar Mukhtar

Awais Hussain

Nafeesa Hamid

Abdul Raouf Qureshi

Nafisa Akhtar

Abdul Karim

Nabeela Ahmed

Iftikhar Kalwal

Language

Abdul Karim

مہاڑی پہاڑی

بولی مہاڑی پہاڑی اے، اِسْنی اے، اُسْنی اے، توبھاڑی اے
ہور پہانویں سمجھن کَنج وی اسکی، مکیی لغنی بہوں پیاری اے
پنجابی نالوں اے لحدری اے، پر ذرا ملمنی نال پوٹھواری اے
آنڈھ گواںڈھ نیاں سب بولیاں وچوں اے نِکڑی چیز نیاری اے
بولنے آلے بہوں اے اسنے پر کھٹ کھٹ کوئی لٹاری اے
جہیڑے وچارے لَکھنے پَئے انہاں ناں کم وی غیر معیاری[1] اے
چِیاں نہ ساہڑی سوادے نی پئی اے تہ نہ کوئی ڈکشناری اے
اس کھاٹے کی پورا کرنے نی اساں ہون کرنی فُلّ تیاری اے
کم اے تھوڑا لماں اے، مکنڑاں نیں سآدیہاڑی اے
شروع کرنا سوخا اے، اوکھا کم رکھنا اسکی جاری اے

---

[1] A point of clarification: غیر معیاری doesn't mean "inferior" but "non-standard," as we have yet to develop a standard form of spellings for native Pahari words

My Pahari

Pahari is my tongue, I love to speak it all the time,
Whatever others may think, to me it's just sublime.
Composed from various neighbouring languages,
With Punjabi and Pothwari it does closely chime.

Whilst speakers of it are many, writers only a few,
Very few are established, most – like me – are new.
Having no standard alphabet or dictionary of spellings,
It's no surprise even the best writing looks a bit askew.

To address this issue, we've just started a new project,
Creating a Roman Pahari alphabet is its primary object.
Soon our kids will be able to write their own language
And it could even become a school curriculum subject!

Bōli

Awais Hussain

بولی
کیتاں لکھنے آں
ایہ سوال کری گئے
جواب میں دیاں
پر مہاڑے خیال مری گئے
میں چاہنساں کہ لکھاں
پر لفظ نہی اچھٹے
جینو مہاڑی منگی وی
تے انگلیاں کمبیٹیاں
انہاں قلم پوری وئی
تے کالی سیاہی نکلنی اے
چٹے سفید ورقے پر
اندروں دلے نی بھڑاس نکلنی اے
لاہو مہاڑیاں ناڑیاں چ وسنا
جسے چ اگے پچھے گسنا
سروں گھنی پیرے جیاں نسنا
سنو تے سہی تے میں دسناں
زینے چ بہوں ساریاں سوچاں
کھیتاں تے مٹھیاں
پر اج لکھائی وچ پہلی واری
اپنی بولی چ کیتاں

Bōli

Bōli
Kiyāñ likhne āñ
Ey sawāl kari gey
Jawāb meiñ dyāñ
Par mhāre khyāl mari gey
Meiñ chāhṇañ ke likhāñ
Par lafz ni achhne
Jeeñv māri sukkivi
Tey angliāñ kambniāñ
Unāñ qalam pōri vi
Kāli siyāhi nikalni eh
Chiṭṭey safaid varqeh par
Andrūñ diley ni bharās nikalni eh
Lowū mhāriyāñ nāriyāñ ch vasna
Jismeh ch aggeh pichheh gasna
Sirūñ kinni pehrāñ jiyāñ nasna
Suno teh seyhi meiñ dasnañ
Zaine-ch bhouñ sāreañ sōchāñ
Khaṭṭiyāñ teh miṭṭhiyañ
Par aj likhai vich pehli vāri
Apni bōlich kittiyāñ

Mother Tongue

Why do we write?
They have asked,
For me to answer,
But my thoughts have passed.
I want to write.
But words don't come to me.
My tongue is dry,
And my fingers tremble.
They are holding a pen:
Black ink flows out
Onto white paper
And my heart's feelings flow from inside.
Blood flows in my veins
It flows around my body.
It runs from head to toe.
Listen, and I will tell.
In my mind are so many thoughts.
Sour and sweet.
But to today for the first time
I've written them in my own mother tongue.

Zaban Apni

Nafeesa Hamid

1. Zabaana nya seeriyahn
Ammi abba kamahn vich Engrizi bolneh
Asah ne kara'ch apni zabaan neh gahneh
Customer achneh doodh paper theh
BELL salaam deni, KARNI DING DONG DING
Swap karoh, un counter neh picha
Engrizi nah homework dasoh abu ki
Friend ai tha fir zabaan aur kij banthi
Un kehl banthi Alum Rockyyy ni Engrizi
Boloh: Burr-min-humm neh lohk sideh
Bareh ya nikeh, Saadeh saadeh
Bohlneh BAB BAB BAB BAB BAB
DUCK tha DERBY lahkeyahn ni hosi

2. Mangethar
schoola thu baad sareh jireh miki paheh
Quran paak madrasseh'ch parai kithi
Jee hah, Kashmir neh grahn vich, Surooh
Eh saari zabaan, eh saara grahn Alum Rock
Thu grahn vich pehda oi seh?
AI AI MANGETHAR
Sachi sach ba!
Bil kol! meh boli yahn
Mangethar kaptha kah ohna
thwareh ammi abba vi ni sun othaiyeh pehda oy?
oh vi ohsan mangethar-freshie, nah?
AI AI NAH JI NAH
NAH?

AI AI Oh tha ithaiyeh pehda oi, HEARTLANDS
Maareh nani naana vi, mareh sareh khadaan
AI AI I can't believe you are freshy!
Raath kini tha freshy freshy bantha mara jisum
Asahn sai British ahn akhni
Asahn ni sach sachi citizenship

3. Zabaan apni
Apni zabaan bohl na haq bunna
Nah osra tha ni, osra khaali kaar boloh
School tha maseethi khaali Urdu
Kaar ammi abba seekhaneh
Urdu Urdu kohshush karo Urdu
Lawan ni saalan akho, janaani ni aurat
Apni zabaan choroh, Urdu boloh
Un bohlna bil kol mushkal oi gya
Zabaan maari
Apni
Zabaan thwaari
Thwaari

My Language

1. tongues and ladders
mum and dad talk English at work
but inside our home, our language sings
customers arrive for milk and papers
bell gives salaam with a DING DONG DING
Behind the counter we swap easy
Abu wants to see my English homework
My friend comes, turns my tongue strange again
We play in Alum Rock's English
Say it loud: Burrr-min-hum folk are soft
Elders, youngers – pure as Kashmiri villagers
Here they say BAB BAB BAB BAB BAB
Duck must be from the tribes of Derby

2. Freshies
After school every kid I knew learned Quran
Paak at madrassah's, I tell my friend I was born
In Kashmir, upon the Quran, yeah, a village, Surooh
Now this is my tongue, this is my village, B8 Rock
She doesn't believe me. You – born in a village??
Oi oi – watch out, we got a mangether in our midst
Tell me the truth, really are you really
Of course, I spoke up, of course that's where
I was born. What did I know about fresh mangthar
Weren't your parents born there too?
They must be freshie-mangethar too, I retaliate
Oh, no no no no my friend, she goes
No?
Nah, they were born here, in Heartlands like me
My nan, grandad – in fact my whole family were

Shaaaaame, I can't believe you are a freshy!
Overnight, freshy freshy became my flesh
She says, we are real British, we got citizenship
More truer than yours – fake British you're fresh

3. My Tongue
Learning my tongue was absolute, non-negotiable
I learned, not like that, only like that at home
At school and madrassah, only Urdu is palatable
In our home, mum and dad teach us
Urdu Urdu, best to learn Urdu, this is better for you
Speak saalan not laawan, speak aurat not janaani
Leave your tongue at home, attach your Urdu tongue
My tongue is tied in every language now, speechless
My tongue is mine
Your tongue is yours.

Zubaan

Nafisa Akhtar

Zubaan bara safar kitha si
Lokan samjya bara kam dehsi

Languages have travelled far and wide, people thought they'd wear them with pride

Khud ni or Apni zubaan ni yaad kuj patha vi ni

I don't really remember my language, I don't really know much either

Akhnay san school vich angrayzi sikhi ja, kam dehsi

They'd say learn English at school, with it you'll go far

Kar vich Pahari thaki suni teh boli ja, changa sillah

but at home "look, listen, speak" Pahari, with it you'll be a "star"

Sirf maseethi vich arbi Quran parri ja, zubaani vi yaad karri ja, Rabb raazi ohsi

Only at mosque read the Quran in Arabic, even memorise it, with it you'll be in the Lord's good books

Urdu vich likhna ni achna? The apne ap ki parya likhya samjhne

"You don't know how to write Urdu? And you call yourself book smart?"

Huun zubaan kuthe kam dehsi? Jawaan hoya the har cheez pulli gyi?

Now where will language get you? You've grown up only to forget everything?

Saarya ni ghallan suni suni the
Jeev apni tehzabaan vi nal, parshani vich passi gyi, huun zubaan kuthe kharsi?

Spending my life listening to everyone, my tongue as well as my language are mute, now where will language take me?

Imran Hafeez

(Punjabi and English interpretation of my father's
ghazal- dekhe hain jo kwhab likh rahe hain)

تکے جیڑے خواب نے او لکھنے پے اں
اکھاں دے عذاب نے او لکھنے پے اں

کلیجے اپر گزری جیڑی کڑی کڑی
اسنے کج حساب نے او لکھنے پے اں

موسم نئی اے پھلاں نا پر فروی
دیوانیاں کول غلاب نے او لکھنے پے اں

عشقے نے اک ای دو لفظ لکھی تے
بس ہجر نے باب نے او لکھنے پے اں

نفرتاں نے سبک پلائی کے اگے
اک تازہ نصاب اے او لکھنے پے اں

We pen the words to write of dreams
and suffering we've seen
To Share the stories captured through eyes
And reflect on what has been

We write of a thought that journeys
From hope and back and forth from our fears
Will we fulfil a promise to the faithful
Still remains unclear
We write of a place that connects our hearts
Up in the city where we know we belong
And of a need to fight for our voice and right

Up in the city now it's time, it's been too long
We write of our losses it eases the pain
And helps sort the confusion to draw some sense
The shackles of society constantly squeezing on limbs
And the people who choose to live in pretence!
And now we write of new beginnings
Overcoming the lessons of hate
We pen the words to write of dreams and
We pen the words to write our fate.

Tongue

Nabeela Ahmed

جیبوا پر قابو رکھنا کن اے؟

Who controls their tongue?

کمزور، غریب، محتاج
ڈرنے بچے، ڈرنیاں جنانیاں

The weak, poor, dependent
scared children, fearful women

ملک کوئی وی وہے
قوماں نا اہ سانجھا قنون

Whichever the country
nations share the rule

جسنی جیب پر ہی وی
اسنی جیبو کھلی وی

Whosevers pocket is full
their tongue is free

بریڈ فورڈ زباناں اشنیاں

زور و زور پوری دنیا چوں

مرنے واسطے

شاہد اتھے نی مٹی بہووں کوملی سی

اللہ سوہنے ہر ملکھے نے

بندے اسنے نال بنائے

Mother tongues come to Bradford
In droves, from around the globe
To die
Perhaps the earth from here
Is extra soft
Allah made people
Of all countries with this

Mari Zaban

Farah Nazir

mari zabān-ne lafs
unanay kahaniya bojo
Pukka teh dard ne
par chai teh āin
platey, shāti
sāri jīva ne vich
Sare pinde ne vich
Sare bakse ne vich
pariya puro mor lawae teh ain
take kaita te tavi
sari zabān jini ae
alni te badli jani ae
dar hov ne nāl
havā te lada ne nāl
shadiā te janāze ne nāl
sari zabān ni marni
akhnay ān
sari zabān ni marni
par shadiā karniā
maze nāl welcome karni ae
naviā galā
pichhle ne nāl
o sawad asāī chakhni ae
valet ne lāle
ikh ikh gara nal
sari jiv, sukhni ni ae
ikh ikh lafs nal
sari jiv chakhni ae

navay jamlay
pichlay naal
jisra sari niki bolni ae
I'm gunning the atta
zabana malai teh jori teh
sari zabaan navia habra sanani eh

ikh ikh lafs
Pound town cone ki
balani eh andar
Jisra ikh ikh mujwan ki Balayna

Balani eh pichleh zabana-nay
zay zabar teh pesh navya nay nal
Kitnia dunya sari zaban vich pirni an
teh asa e zabana jiv per lay teh
kitnay dunya pirnay a

My Language

The words of my language;
listen to their stories
They came packed and
sealed across the mountains
their pain and sorrow
wrapped up into
our tongues
our bodies
our suitcases
In the face of it all,
our language is still alive
She moves and changes with
dar and hof
Dreams and love
Weddings and funerals
Our language does not die
They say:
Our language does not die
But she welcomes the new
with the old in the most
delicious ways –
a delicacy tasted in our very
mouths
The mouths of British lalay
Our tongue doesn't parch
With one word after another
Our tongue doesn't parch
Our tongue elegantly dances
and flirts from one frequency
to another – tasting new

meanings with ancient ones
Like our little girl says:
"I'm gunning the atta"
Languages pieced and
blended
She becomes one

Welcoming new meanings
into organisms,
decorating them with ancient
grammar
Each one is given its own
affix,
a new pattern,
form,
meaning.
Pound Town cone-ki
Blended into one
Connecting and unlocking
new realities,
birthing new ideologies,
giving way and space to
ancient ones –
we travel the world.

Third Space

Sarah Shehr Birmingham

Nafeesa Hamid

sarah shehr, Birmingham
sareh grahn Alum Rock paleh ohne sun Irish
ohna neh mulka vich vi gai Engrehz ni empire
jis vela ahsa Kashmiri ai yah, soneh neh ticket labeh
naana neh prah Sheffield ni factory'ch kam kitha
naana Kashmir thu khali chapal, safehd salwar-kameez
lay tha ai sun, coat boot maloh kohni – sardi na ka patha?
assah ki ka patha si kithna kaura mohsam, kithna nehra
itha ohsi, thahnyeh assa coat'ah ni business karoh chalai
naani, ammi, bareh khala, nikyah khala kapreh seeran
factory ala acha jummeh , unseerth bagah neh baagah
janaaniya aurtthan kandi par Brother machinah swel
kini jiyahn raatha thuk, ohna neh anghva marooran ohn
factory ala ughleh jummeh muri acha coatahn vasteh
doh, thra pound ohna ki laban, M&S aur BHS behchan
viyahn pound.
paleh veeka Englend'vich nana gai factori'onch
khaali doh engrizi lafz tha imaan naal – JOB PLEASE
mareh abu jaan taxi thu baad, video ni shahp khareedi neh
usne thu baad, abu neh paper shahp nya havah chaliyahn
asah ne shahpeh ne paar Brookhill Pub ohni si chrohkni
pub band oi markets kuleh. Markets doh meeneh
bas doh meeneh kuleh, meh andar vi na gai
ohn masjid vastheh planning approval labi
eh sara grah shuruh oiya, Dadyal aal, pur itha Birmingham
Alum Rock - naana akhneh - sai kan koli tha bojoh bacheh
eh sara grahn - chnage bacheh ammi aba neh
kohl rehne, boh dohr kadha vi na jai - kah lohr?

khaar a - kohl kohl saareh roh, ik doweh ni dehk baal karoh
zindagi mushkal kaliyohn khaar a - sab koch mili jaana
shukar Allah asah itha grahn banaya, pyaareh Alum Rock vich
Asahn grahn neh bandeh gutteh rakeh, baradari rakhi Alum Rock'ch.

Our Big City, Birmingham

In our village, Alum Rock, first came the Irish
The English empire invaded their land too
Then we Kashmiri's arrived with our golden tickets
Grandad's brother worked metal in Sheffield factories
Grandad arrived with sandals and white salwar kameez
This is how he dressed, no coat no boots – what did we know
Of the cold?
He said he knew nothing of frosts, never seen such long dark
The cold inspired a coat sewing business from the living room
Nan, mum, mum's sisters took a Brother sewing machine each
Factory-man came on Fridays, with bags and bags of fabrics
The women pressed the Brother machines from crack of dawn
Til dusk their spines, fingers cramping and knotting hours by
Factory-man would return the Friday next, for coat collection
£2 or 3 for them, M&S or BHS would sell for £100 plus
In his first month in England, grandad went from factory to factory with only two English words – JOB PLEASE
In our first year back in England, dad left taxi for a VHS store
After he sold it, dad then dreamed of opening his own shop
Back then, we had the Brookhill Pub across our shop

When the pub closed in 2010, some markets took over
They lasted two months, I didn't even get to go in
Now planning permission is granted for a new mosque
Now this is really our village, like Dadyal, here in Brum
Alum Rock – grandad says – open your ears good and listen

This is our village now, children are blessed when they stay
Close to their parents, close to the family of migrating blood
Stay close to each other, no need to go too far – what's the need
Home is staying near each other, looking out for the other
This life is a hard life, everything you'll ever need is right here
Endless thanks for what our Lord helped us build
Our beloved Alum Rock kept our kinship ties strong seas apart
Our village of unity in our beloved Alum Rock

Pakistan naa Sair

Kausar Mukhtar

Pyu asaaN a ki kharyaah Pakistan
Asah taki sunhi theh saara
Rey ghay araan parshaan
Taki keh asaN ki dukandaar keemataN chaaran
Budeh teh keh jawaan akkhaa maaran
Aakhnayn kurriyah walyti khraab an saariyah
Apnayaa putrah nih khabar koy ni
Jinnah khotiyah theh bakriyah naal
Pataa ni kitniyah raatan guzariyaan
Pakistan eh mulk muslamaana nah
Meh bass takya utheh kam shaitaana nah

Trip to Pakistan

Father took us to Pakistan
We couldn't believe our eyes and ears
The prices increased when we entered the bazaar
Men young an old made vulgar gestures
"You know what British girls are like"
Their minds and thoughts resident in gutters and sewers,
What expectation could then we
Have about their actions
They are happy to turn a blind eye when their sons
Spend many a passionate night with donkeys and goats
Pakistan is a country of Muslims we're told
But everywhere I looked I saw the devil's work

an N represents an N sound that is nasal and partially silent

پہچان

Awais Hussain

پہچان ساڑی بڑی عجیب اے
میں اِتھے ولایت نے پیدائش آں
اِتھے جمیاں، اِتھے پڑھیاں، اِتھے رہناں
پر والدین مہاڑے چکسواری نے پیدائش ان
اُتھے جَمَن، اُتھے پلَن، اُتھے رَسَن
تے فِر آئی گئَن اِتھے
جسرح کوئی ہانڈی رِنے پکائے او
اُسرح اساں نی پہچان بنی گئی اے
بے شمار چیزاں نال
تھوڑا جیا لُون بسارے کُجھ سبزیاں
جسرح تھوڑی جئی انگریزی وی
پہاڑی پوٹھوہاری وی، تے اردو وی،
تے اوراں شےاں وی
یا جسرح پتنگ اے
بہوں سارے رنگ ان
سُونے، پِیلے، ساوے، نیلے
پر اساں دو رنگاں نے بشکار آں
جسرح اساں پُورے سُونے وی ناں
تے پُورے پِیلے وی ناں

اس اُسنے درمیان آں
اِک پیر مہاڑا ولایت وچ اے، بریڈفورڈ شیر
تے دُونا پیر اپنے گراں چ، بے تے باوے نے کہاڑ
اِک پیر اِتھے رار
اِک پیر اُتھے سمندروں پار

تے فِر میں سوچناں
کِس رح کھلاں

Pehchān

Pehchān sāri bari ajeeb jiy eh
Meiñ itheh walait ni pedaish añ
Itheh jamyañ, itheh parhyañ, itheh rehnañ
Par waldain māre Chakswari ne pedaish an
Uttheh jammeyn, utheh palleyn, utheh reyn,
Teh fir eyi geyn itheh
Jisra koi handi rinny pakāny o
Usra asañ ni pehchan bani giy eh
Be shmār cheezañ nāl
Thora jya loon basār teh sabziyāñ
Jisra thori jiy ingrezi vi,
Pahari-Pothwari vi, teh urdu vi, teh or sheyāñ vi

Ya jisra peeng eh,
Bouñ sarey rang an,
Suwey, peeley, sāvey, neeley,
Par asañ do rangāñ ne bishkar añ
Jisra asañ pūrey suwey vi nañ
Teh pūrey peeley vi nañ
As us ne darmiyān añ
Ik pēr mara walaitich eh, Bradford sher
Teh duwah per apne garāñch, bey teh bāvey ne kār
Ik pēr itheh rār
Ik pēr utheh samundruñ pār

Teh fir meiñ sochnañ
Kisra khallañ

Identity

Our identity is quite peculiar.
I was born here in England,
Born here, studied here, live here.
But my parents were born in Chakswari,
Born there, raised there, lived there,
And then they came here.
Our identity has been made like just
as how you make a curry -
With many different ingredients:
A little salt and spice, some vegetables,
Like a little English, some Pahari-Pothwari too,
and a bit of Urdu, among other things.
Or like a rainbow
With many different colours:
Red, yellow, green, blue.
But we are in the middle of two colours;
Not quite red,
Nor quite yellow,
But we are somewhere in-between.
One of my feet is in England, in Bradford.
The other is in our village, at our grandparents' home.
One foot here,
One foot there across the seas.

And then I think to myself:
How do I stand?

شرمندہ

Imran Hafeez

ساف زایر اکھاں نے سامنے مُسلماناں نہ ایہہ ہو ریا قتلِ عام
پر اساں نی نذر ناساں کو لوں اگے وی نہ لانگی سکی۔
کجلنے جوگے کیڑیاں مکوڑیاں ار ہی گیاں

اس توں اگّے ہور میں کہہ سمجھاں، کہہ سمجھیا انھا لکی۔
جینے سامنے باکی سب کچھ مزید آوا را اگردگی لگنی
اساں نیاں اکھاں گواہ بنی گئیاں فو نہ نیاں سکرینانیاں کہہ کج نی دسیا؟
کے کفا آیاں ار ہمیشہ شرمندہ لکھے جاساں اساں؟
بارگاواں تک کے سمجنے اں اوہ فریاداں نہ پہونچسن؟
اک فلسطینی ماں نی خوفناک چیخ تے پکار!

گود یچ آپنیے بچے نی باڈی نے گوشتے نے چھتڑیے پلیٹی
منّج بخری نہ جائیں ماڑا پتر۔
شہیدے کی دینی اک آخری پیغام۔
پہونچے تے اللہ نے جیب کی دسیں اساں اپر کیتی گئی دہشت تے بر ہی تے آکھیں
سرکار، سارے تکنیے رہے تماشا

- 39 -

Sharminda

Daylight murder of Muslims,
Yet we don't see past the end of our nose!
Thought of as nothing more than bugs to be squished!
Everything in comparison is but an insignificant galivant.
Our eyes bear witness to the things we've seen on our phone screens.
Like the people of Kuffa are we destined for an eternal guilt?
Do we think their prayers won't breach the heavens?
The soul tingling screams of a Palestinian mother!!
She carefully gathers the torn pieces of flesh, what's left of her child
And utters a parting complaint to the martyr…
When you get there, make sure to tell Allah's beloved,
What injustice has been done to us!
And tell him- they all just stood and watched!!

Abdul Karim

ولائتی جینڑاں

جہڑے پہلے پہلے وچ ساہڑے لوک ولائت آئے
کجھ پُچھی تے خوش ہوئے ، کجھ وچارے پچھتائے
جہڑے تے انہاں وچوں عمروں پکروڑے سن
اوتے اتھے ڈاہڈے کمے تھوں نہیں کہوڑہائے
تے جہڑے لوبکے بچے ماؤں پیونے لاڈلے سن
او ہفتہ فیکٹری وچ لائی تے دُکھے نال کرلائے
بڑیاں کولوں ڈری تے کمے پر تے او جانے رے
پر دِلے وچوں وازاں لِکن : ہائے او مہاڑیئے مائے

کجُھ اتھے اُچھی اپنے لوکاں کولوں چھپی گئے
فر بلیں بلیں اتھے نیں ماحول وچ کھپی گئے
کجھ اس اوپرے معاشرے تھوں تپی گئے
فر سب کجھ چھوڑی تے ملکھے نا راہ کپی گئے
کجھ بے شرم بنی تے ساریاں حداں ٹپی گئے
فر آپنا قصور وی کئے ہور نے سر تھپی گئے

کجاں صبر نا پیالہ پیتا ، تے سارے دکھ چلھے
جتھے تک ہوئی سکیا ، کیتے اک دوئے نال پلھے
کمھٹے رہنڑیں ، کمھٹے بہنڑیں ، کمھٹے سینڑیں

تے نہ ہی باہر جانڑیں سن او کدے کلھے
اپنے نکیاں نکیاں کھراں نے انہاں
پر ہی شوڑے سارے کنٹھاں پچھے
جوان جان چڑھی گئے اپر الکاں جیاں
بڈھے ٹھیڑے ٹلھی گئے وچ سلّھے

Foreign Living

Of the first wave of our people arriving in the UK,
Some were really happy, others full of regret.
Those who were of mature years,
Hard work did not cause them fret.
But the younger ones, darlings of their parents,
After a week of work, became very upset.
They kept going to work, fearful of the elders,
And called their mums[2], whom they could not forget.

Some overcame the elders' blockade,
And effectively turned renegade.
Some got fed-up of this alien culture they couldn't understand,
So, they abandoned everything and went back to motherland.
Some found excuses to exceed all boundaries
Blaming it on the elders and their beloved foundries.

Some remained steadfast, accepting the hardships,
Supporting each other, nurturing new friendships.
Living together, talking together,
Working together, walking together.
With new arrivals, their small houses were packed,
No space was empty; every nook and cranny were stacked.
The youngsters went up and filled the attics,
Elders settled in the cellar, being pragmatics.

---

[2] Apparently, people of every race and culture instinctively call to their mothers in extreme distress.

تربی جغہ

Nabeela Ahmed

لوک تساں نال ملنے نی، ناں شکلاں، ناں رنگ
ناں مذہب، ناں رسماں، نا جین ہکھے جیا، ناں مرن

سدا لوک یاد دلانے رہنہیں کہ تساں توں پہلے
لوک خوش سن، چوری چکاری، ڈاکہ بجھیانی سی

آپہی گڈ اہمگرینٹ ثابت کرنیا، آپنیا تھوں نفرت دسہی
فر وی اہک دماکے نی غل اے، ہر بندہ فرمگنا اے ثبوت

وہیاں سالاں بعد، اہ ہی چلہی چلہی ملکھے چ گئی
اپنا رہنا ہی کن اے؟ اک بچی سن، او بولے

بیلہ تکی یاد اے؟ او سہونے دیہارے سن تیجے
گراں پرہے وہے سن اپنیاں لوکاں نال

ہر بچے بڈھے کی بندہ جانناسی
کدھے چوڑی چکاری نا ناں وھی نی سی بجھیا

پہناں پراواں آڑ رہنے سن ساڑھے، دکھ منڈھ کرنے سن
ہن تہ پتہ نی کدھرے کدھرے نے لوک ہن

ٹرک پرھنے تہ کہار خالی کری اولے جانے
اپنا گراں اوپرا لگنا ے، کوئی اپنابندہ اہیہی کوئی نی

ملی اے واز جانی پہچانی لگی، ہر بڈھی تہ
بڈھے گورے نی واز ! ملی چپ لگی گئی

ترہی جغہ
ہر جغہ ہونی اے؟

- 45 -

A Place in Between

People you once knew are now strangers,
No familiar faces, no colours,
No religion, no traditions,
No shared way of life, no common death.

They always remind you that before you,
People were happy, there was no theft,
No robbery, no crime.

They prove themselves as good immigrants,
By despising those like them.
Still, when disaster strikes,
Everyone must prove themselves again.

After twenty years of bearing this, she returned 'home'

There was no one left there, just a grandma

She whispered, "Do you remember?
Those were the golden days,
Villages filled with our own,
Every child, every elder known to each other.

No theft, no fear, no strangers.
Brothers and sisters stood together,
Sharing joy and sorrow alike.

But now, who knows who anyone is?"

Trucks arrive,
They clear the houses,
They claim our villages as theirs,
And there is no one left who is truly ours.

A voice calls out—familiar, yet distant.
Every old white man and woman's voice?
I fall silent.

A place in between—
Does it exist everywhere?

Tayrah Saal

Kausar Mukhtar

Mae ni Mae hathaN saryah wichu gudiyah khoy theh kiyah
   shaddi niyah mehndi layah
Gurbat dur karneh wasteh mah pyu theh penha prawah niyah judai-ah paiyaaN
"Bay mari dholi tornayaN tusah akhyaa si teeyay twarah janaza wapis acheh"
"Maraa ajji barrah roya si, mari bachi bhu nikki eh"
Walyat neh lalach vich uwaaN na bachpan kohn
   oyah weh
"Nikka praa mara, khat phori theh turna si jileh meh England
   gei sah"
Fir mil-yah jileh veeyah saalah nah si, "meh tussah ki koni peshanyaN Bi",
MaryaaN teh door gayaa vich farak koyni, dholi theh janazeh
   nah vih farak koy ni

Age 13

Mother oh mother why did you snatch the doll from my hands
and replace it wedding mendhi
To remove me from poverty you separated me from parents
and siblings
When bidding farewell to my wedding carriage you told me
not to return other than in a
shroud
My father cried terribly, my daughter is too young for marriage
The lure of England destroyed many an innocent childhood
My youngest brother was barely walking when I left for
England
I met him again when he was 20 years old, "I
don't recognise
you sis!"
There was no difference between
death and distance
There was no difference between the wedding carriage
and
the coffin

Nature

Maari Sehli

Nafisa Akhtar

ماڑی سہیلی
میں ہک سوہنی جی سہیلی رکھی اے
ہر دیہاڑی راتی گارڈنے وچ کھلتی ہوئی اے
چڑیاں سفید ٹالیاں تے نیلے پتلے پتے نیں
اوچیاں ٹالیاں اس کریں نی راضی رکھنی اے
اسنیاں ٹالیاں چیرے ہونیاں
میں سوچنی اہ کے ماڑھے کار کی جھپی دینا چاھنی اے
میں اپلے ویندے توں واپس اسکی تکنی رھنی اہ
تکی تے بڑا سکون اچھنا
میں اسکی ناہ نی دتا
جہاں اور درخت میکی اللہ دتا
لغنا اے کے ماڑھے کہرے نیاں غلاں سننی رھنی اے
ھلنی چلنی اے اپنی رائی دسنی اے تے غل بات واپس کرنی
چیلے ماڑا دل تھوڑا ھونا
بڑا حوصلہ دینی اے
آخنی اے کے ماڑھے ار مضبوط بن ھمت نہ ھار
جیڑا موسم اچھسی توں اپنیاں جڑاں کی نہ مار
آخنین ہر شئے گواہی دیسی
اے درخت اللہ میکی دیتا

تے جیڑی چیز خدا کولوں منگسو سو کجھ دیسی
جیے حضور پاک نی درخت محبت نل جنت پوہنچی
دعا اے کے اے درخت وفاداری نل میکی جنت کھڑسی وسیلہ بنسی
اس شہرے وچ ایہے جے درخت کافی این
پر اجکل گارڈنے وچ ایہے جی سہلی کن رکھنا اے؟

My Friend

I've got a beautiful Friend
Day & night there she stands in the garden
With white branches, and leaves yellowy green she stands tall
Watching over the house an all
Her widespread branches like arms reaching for the house, enveloping it in her loving embrace
From the upstairs window I see it all, the view, & the smiles she brings to my face
I haven't named her, because, for me, she is from God's grace
It seems she hears all the chaos that goes on at my place
Her branches swaying to and fro, telling me what she thinks about all the fiasco
Whenever I grow weary, she consoles me so
Saying; "be like me, strong and resilient, whatever the weather, don't be unsteady on your feet"
They say every living thing will speak one day, and she too will speak for me
This tree is my heavenly gift
Whatever we ask from God, He grants it swift
So, if the tree that wept out of love reached his heavenly abode: the best of states
I can ask that this tree's loyalty will be a means of me reaching those heavenly gates
You see, there are many similar trees in this city, but who has this one? A companion in the garden...who keeps friends like these?

اٹھ پہر

Awais Hussain

سویرے سویرے سرگی الے
دے نن ٹُکر بانگاں
بندے جاگنا شروع اُوئی جانے
مسیتی چ دے ن آزاناں
سُتّے سارے جاگنے
تے پڑھن فِر نمازاں
چِڑیاں وی اپنے عبادت کرن
کٹھیاں اُوئی تے ڈارنیاں
دَیں نکلنا شروع اونا
زِمیناں لوہ لویل اوئی جانیاں

بندے کماں چ پائی جانے
مال مویشہ چارنے تے گھنی جانے
پُوری دیہاڑ لائی جانے
تے شامی واپس مُڑنے

نماشاں ویلے
دَیں ٹلنا
چِڑیاں کَٹھیاں اچھنیاں
ڈاراں نے ڈار
شام پئی جانی اے
گُپ نیرا اُوئی جانا یا
تے کُفتاں اُوئی جانیاں

بِنڈے چیں چیں کرنے
تِڑیاں بولنیاں
ٹنانے اُڈرنے تے چمکنے
اسماناں پر تارے تارے اُوئی جانے

sveyreh sveyreh sargee eleh
deyneyn kukkar bāngāñ
bandey jāgna shuruh uwi jāney
maseetich deyn azānāñ
suttey sārey jāgney
teh paṛhneyn fir namāzāñ
chiriāñ vi apny ibādat karan
gaṭṭhiyāñ uwi teh ḍārniyāñ
deyñ niklna shuruh ona
zameenāñ loh laveel uwi jāniyāñ

bandy kammāñ-ch peyi jāney
māl mweysha chārney teh ghini jāney
poori diyāṛ leyi jāney
teh shāmi vapus murney

namāshāñ veyleh
deyñ talna
chiriāñ gaṭṭhiāñ acchniāñ
ḍarāñ ne ḍār

shām piy jāni eh
gup neyra uwi jāna ya
teh kuftāñ uwi jāniyāñ

binḍey cheeñ cheeñ karney
triḍḍiyāñ bolniyāñ
tanāney uḍārney teh chamkneyn
asmānāñ-par tārey tārey uwi-jāney

Early in the morn,
The cockerels crow,
And people start to rise,
And in the mosques, they give the call to prayer.
All those asleep, rise
And read their prayers,
And the birds worship too,
Flying together in flocks.
The sun starts to emerge,
And the lands are filled with light.

People start to work,
They go to herd their animals,
They work all day,
And return at night.

At dusk,
The sun descends,
Birds gather together,
Flock upon flock.

Night falls,
And it becomes dark.
The night settles in.

The crickets chirp,
And the grasshoppers click.
The fireflies fly and glow,
and the sky is filled with stars.

Green Bradford

Nabeela Ahmed

اساں پھلاں نال پیار اپنے نکھے جے گارڈنے چوں سکھیا
امی ابو نے گلاب تہ پودنے نی خوشبو اساں نا حصہ اے

We learnt to love flowers from out tiny garden
Fragrance of mum and dad's roses and mint is a part of us

گریٹ ہارٹن پارک کے چ اجی کھڑنے سن
پدیاں مچھلیاں پورنے ساں ڈمبے چوں

Aji took us to Great Horton Park
We fished for tiny fish at the pond

نارتھ کلف پارک کے چ ابو جی بینچے پر بہی
اپنیاں نکلی لتاں لائی شورنے سن
تہ سوٹا لانے سن بینسن تہ ھیجزنا

At Northcliff park dad would sit on a bench, taking off his prosthetic legs and enjoying long drags of Bensons & Hedges

شپلی گلین پاپا کھڑنے سن، پکنک واسطے
اساں نا شہر پہاڑی شہر اے، اساں پہاڑی بندیاں آڑ

Pop took us to Shipley Glen, for a picnic
Our city is a hill city, like us hilly people

مارہ نکہ کچھنا اے چپہ چپہ اپنی سائنکلا پر

ویسی پارک، ہارلڈ پارک، ڈیوزبڑی سائیکل وے

My youngest covers every inch on his bike
Wibsey Park, Harold Park, the Dewsbury track

بڑے کی چڑ اے پارکاں نال۔ پر ستیہا وی جاغی پینا اے

جے نا کہو، جوڈی وڈز، اوگڈن واٹرز، سالٹئیر، خاورتھ

The older one isn't into parks, but will rise at anytime
If you mention Judy Woods, Ogden Waters, Saltaire, Haworth

اساں نے دور وچ باہر جانا ہونی سی ٹریٹ

بچیاں کی سخایا اے، قدرت وچ پھرنا

ٹریٹ نی، جانی تہ روح، دوہاں نا بہترین علاج اے

In our times going out was seen as a treat
We've taught our children that wandering in nature
Is not a treat, but the best medicine for your body and soul

اُلّو ناں پَٹھا
Abdul Karim

میں سویلے سویلے پارکے وچ ٹُرناں لگا جاناں ساں
آپے نال کوئی دِلے وچ گلاں باناں جاناں ساں

اک تُھوڑے کولوں ننگنیاں تھوڑی کھڑ کھڑ ہوئی
میں کھلی تے بُجھیا تے فِر تھوڑی جی پَھڑ پَھڑ ہوئی

ایچرے نی اتھوں وچوں اک پنچھیروں اُٹھی نَٹھا
میں سوچیا اے کہہ لوڑناں سی اِتھے اُلّو ناں پَٹھا

او وچارہ زخماں نے دَردے نال بلکل چُور ہویا وا سی
اُڈرنا تے ہَیدر ری گیا او دوڑنیاں وی مجبور ہویا وا سی

بل کری تکیا تے او کسے پرندے ناں نِکا جا بچہ سی
می کی پتہ لگی گیا جے مہاڑا پہلا خیال شاید سچا سی

جہڑا مہاڑے کولوں ٹھوڑے چوں لِکڑی تے نٹھا سی
او اُچے بُوٹے پروں اک اَلڑے وچوں پیہیاں ٹُٹھا سی

زخمی ہوئی گیا سی تے وچارہ ٹرناں وی مَٹھا مَٹھا سی
او سچے مچے چِٹا تے سوہنا اُلو ناں اک نِکا جاپٹھا سی

فِر او اک کیڑا تکلی دوڑیا تے فٹا فٹ اسکی چینجے وچ پوڑیاس
تھوڑا جا اسناں گاٹا مروڑیاس، فِر او جینا ای کھائی شوڑیاس

تک تکنیاں اپروں اک لُوہندی انی چھاپہ ماریا
پنجے وچ اُلو ناں پٹھا چائی تے آپے نال اڈاریا

دور بوٹے نی چوٹی پر اپنے الڑے وچ اسی بہیا لیا
جِتھے فِر اس اُلوے نے پٹھے کی بوٹی بوٹی کری ٹھا لیا

قدرت ناں اے سخت قانوں سارے بندے جانڑ جاؤ!
جہڑا لبنا اے کھانڑے جاؤ یا فِر ۔۔۔۔ آپوں کھانڑ جاؤ!

- 61 -

Son of an Owl

I was in the local park on my morning stroll,
Trying to keep the burst of ideas under control.
Passing by a bush, I thought I heard a rattle,
Listening carefully, it was more of a crackle.

A bird emerged from the bush, trying to run clear,
And I thought: what's this Son of an Owl doing here?
It was badly injured and emitted a sudden squawk.
Let alone flying, this poor thing could hardly walk.

I looked at the chick and thought "Poor little you,"
And my original thought turned to be literally true.
It was hobbling and wobbling but doing its best,
This clumsy fledgling that had fallen from a nest.

It was very confused, hurt, cold, and walking very slowly,
But it was definitely a pretty, white, little son of an owly!
Seeing a little insect, it made a sudden dive,
It held it in its beak, then swallowed it alive!

Just then an eagle swooped and I quicky saw,
It picked up the Son of Owl in its mighty claw.
Off it flew to its perch high up on a very tall tree,
And consumed the Son of Owl with obvious glee.

Natural law says you either beat or be beaten!
To put it more accurately: you eat or be eaten!

Bradford ni Khubsurti

Nafisa Akhtar

May kaafi shehrañ vich ray aye añ par
Bradford ni khūbsurthi koi ohr chīz eh
Asañ ney buzurg apney zameenañ ki chohri the
itheh ni zameen uña ki itheh bulaya
Is pahari lāka na ithna farq ni
Sabz neem rang darkhtañ beyshumār
Gulāb nay būtay, saṭ barka, teh ohr phul kithney rangdār
Keh dasseh banda, pārkañ vich turri teh dimāgh kithna khalqa ohna
Sāf suthri hawā khai teh, Yorkshire ni pāni pē the, vāpas aye janiyeh jawāni

Bradford's Beauty

I've lived in a lot of cities
But the beauty of Bradford is something else
Our elders left their land, and came to this lands calling
This mountainous hilly? land is not much different to theirs
Filled with Green-yellowy leaved trees,
Roses, marigolds and multi coloured flowers
What more can be said about Bradford?
How fresh & lightheaded we get walking through the parks
Breathing in the clean air, drinking Yorkshire water; the pure fountain of youth!

Short Story

Lajj

by Ifikhar Kalwal

لِچ
Iftikhar Kalwal

پینہ کی انہاں دیہاڑیاں چ خورے کہہ ہویا سی ۔ چُپ چُپ رہنی سی ۔ مُنویں اپر مُسکڑی جئی :پتہ لغناں سی اندرو اندر لڈو پُھٹنے۔ شرمانیاں چیلا منویں اگے رکھی مٹھا جیا ہسی یا متھے کی مارا جیا چک ماری مُو اُدھر کری کنی سی۔ جسلے بُوٹیاں اپروں پتر ٹھی پئے، بُوٹے سُکی گے، پینہ ناں مُنہ اسراہ مولے آسی جسراہ بہار اجئے ہُن شروع ہوئی وئے ۔

اصلوں انہاں دیہاڑیاں وچ اُس نی پُھوہ اپنے مڑے فوقے ۔ فاروق واسطے پینہ ناں ساک منگیا سی۔

اے او ویلا سی جسلے تھیاں پُتر ماؤ پُھیو تھوں دوئی نہی سن کرنے ۔ پینہ تے فوقے کدے آپے اسراہ نی غل نی سی کیتی، پر وچوں وچوں دوئے ہک دوئے کی پسند کرنے سن ۔پینہ ناں ابا تے فوقے ناں مانواں چوہدری صابر بڑا نامی گرامی جناں سی ۔ سارا گراں اسنی عزت کرنا سی۔ دِلّے ناں وی چنگا سی پر کوڑا) روئے آلا (بہوں سی۔ کوئی ماڑا کم ٹکے یا غل بُجھے تے رہو وی بہو کرنا سی۔ ساریاں کی پتہ سی ہک واری چوہدری صابر جہڑی غل کری چھوڑے فر اسکی کوئی مکرائی نہی سی سکنا۔ فوقا وی باقیاں ال مانوے کولو ڈرنا سی ۔

فوقے تے پینہ نے کہار کو لو کول سن ۔ ترے چار باڑیاں چھوڑی رار پار۔
فوقی نی اماں پینہ نی پہُوہ، نسرین اجئے ہکے واری پینہ نیں رشتے نی غل کیتی سی۔
اجئے پینہ نیں ابے ہاں نی سی کیتی۔ اُناں آخیا سی سوچی تے باساں ۔

فئروی پینہ نیں پیر زیویں اپر نھی سن لغنے۔ اُسکی اسراہ لغنا سی جسراہ ہو ہک پری ہے
تے اسماناں اپر اُڈرنی ہے پئی ۔ پینہ خیالاں وچ پری ار اسماناں اپر اُڈرنی تے
اصل وچ کھووے اپڑوں پانیے ناں کھڑا چائیاں بہڑے پہوتی تے تکلیاں باوے
پچھجّے پارلے موہڑے آلے ناں مُڑاتے نُہوں جیڑے ولیت ہونے، بہڑے بیٹھے
وے. بل خیر کری پینہ اپنے کم کرن نئی پئی۔ پینہ کی واز آئی چنگا لالا اساں کل فئر
اچھسا ۔ پینہ دِلے وچ سوچیا اج ہوئی جے جُلہے کل خورے کہیاں مُڑسن۔

پینہ اپنے کہارے نیں کماں وچ لغی رہی تے اسنے اماں ابا آپے وچ گُھش گُھش
کرن لغی پے ۔ پینہ نیں ابے اُسنی نکی پہنو جینہ کی آخیا جا، پُہوہ نسرین کی بلائی
آن ۔

فوتے نی اماں سارے کم کاج سٹی سٹائی گولی آر پاپے صابرے نیں کھار پہوتی ۔ راہ اشنیاں کئی خیال آئیں ۔ کج مٹھا کنی اچھا آر ۔

مٹھائی نی تے کہار تھوڑے مخانے سن ، ہووے کنی اچھا آر ۔ لالا آخسن نلوں سخنی اُٹھی آئی ھے ۔ سپنہ دلیچا بھی آٹا گئی سی پئی ۔ فوتے نی اماں خوشی ناں ساس ماری دِلے وچ سوچیا ، ایہہ ماہڑی تھی بُن مہاڑے بہڑے پھریا کرسی. کتنی سوہنی جوڑی ہوسی ، نظر نہ لگے

چوہدری صابر آخن لگا پہنو ٹکی تاں بلایاں جئے ہک صلاح کرنی ایہہ ۔

جی جی لالہ دسو . نسرین بہوں خوش ہوئی وائی لالہ پہلی واری مہاڑے نال وی کوئی صلاح کرن لگے

باوے پھجے ناں مڑاتے نہوں آئے سن ۔ پروین ناں ساک منگیا نیں ۔ اے بجھی فوتے نی اماں ناں موں پھک ہوئی گیا ۔ پنہ نے ہتھ آٹا گھنیاں گھنیاں کھلی گئے ۔ اسکی اسراہ لگا جیڑی پنہ پری بنی وی اسمانے اپر اُڈنی سی پئی ، اُسنے پر کپن گے این تے اسمانے او زیویں اپر ہک جنگلے وچ ٹھی پئی ۔ جنگلے نے چار چوفیرے سمندر ھے تے جنگلے وچ بڑیاں بڑیاں بلائیاں آن جہڑیاں اُسکی کھائی جاسن سپنہ اپنے ابے نی آخری غل بُجی اوے پچھے تے سارے پیورے پکے

کج سن، اس ساکے نال فخر پرانے رشتتے نویں رشتتے ہوئی جا سن ۔ ٹکی میں نکی تہھی ناں رشتہ دئ چھوڑساں

دوئے دیہاڑے پینہ نے ابے زبان دئ چھوڑی ۔
راتیں چوہدری صابرے کی کھرے نے بُن باڑیاں وچ بیٹری نی لائٹ لغنی دسی ۔ کدے لائٹ اسنے کھرے کول اچھئے فخر پشیں مڑی جائے ۔ فخر نیڑے اچھئے فخر پشیں مڑی جائے ۔ چوہدری صابرے بہڑنیاں کج ماری کن اے ہوئے ۔

لائٹ بند ہوئی گئی ۔ پیراں نیں وازاں توں پتا لغنا سی کوئی نسی لمنے آر ٹلھیی گیا ۔ فوقی کی ہمت نہی پئی جنے آپوں جنی مانویں صابرے نال غل کرے ۔ کہار جائی اماں نال بائیس ۔
دو دے دیہاڑے فوقنی اماں اپنے پراہوٗ صابر کول گئی تے بہنیں نال ہی گوکاں ماری رون لغنی پئی ۔ فوقنی اماں اپنے پراہوٗ کولوں ڈرنی سی تاں اُسنے کولوں رون ڈکن نی ہویا ۔ پینہ نی اماں تے ابے دوواں نسرین کولوں پچھیا
کہہ ہویا ہی نسرین خیر تے ایہہ؟
نسرین چنگا چیر ہتکورے پھرنی رہی ۔ فخر ہمت کری آخن لغنی

مہاڑا فاروق آخنا پینہ ناں بیاہ پکھّے نے پوترے نال نہ کرو۔ اُسنے کرتوت نھی چنگے۔
اگے ہک بیاہ کری رہیا۔ اپنے نیڑے نیاں سکیاں وچوں کسے ساک نھی دِتا۔
سارے آخنے نشئی ایہہ
نسرین فےررون نئی پئی۔
مہاڑا پتر آخنا، مانوے کی آخو پینہ ناں بیاہ مہاڑے نال پانوے نہ کرو، پر پہڑے بندے
نیں پلے وی نہ باہنؤ جئے ساری حیاتی زاو تکے
سارے چنگا چپ چپ رے۔ اے اسراہ نی چپ سی جسنے کولوں ڈر لگے۔
آخیر چوہدری صابر بولیا
تُسا کی پتہ ھے سارا ڈڈیال جاناں ھے وائی صابر جہڑی غل کری چھوڑے اُس توں
کدے پچھے نی ہٹیا پانوے جان لگی جائے
چوہدری صابرے پینہ کی ڈولی بھالنیاں آخیا
پتر اجس کہارے تہی نی ڈولی جانی اُٹھوں جنازہ ہی نکلنا۔ پیو نی گلا نی لج رکھیاں۔

منان جہڑا میکسی آخوانا سی، ہک دن سلور ناں لوائے یا سیس، کالا رنگ، بڑیاں
ناساں، سوہبیاں (سرخ) ڈروانیاں اکھاں گلے بڑی ساری زنجیری تے ہک گنے مُرکی
پینہ نیں دلے وچ منان کی پہلی واری تکنیاں ہی ڈر بہی گیا۔

پنہ ولیت اُٹھی آئی۔ ولیت کہہ سی ہوے جنگل سی جسنّے چہ پاسے سمندر سی، جنگلے وحشی درندے اسنّے جسے کپئی کھانیں سن، اسنّے منے اپر کھلوندراں نیں نشان سامنے دِسنے سن، بہناواں اپرتی استری نیں کہنیاں نشان سن جغہ سن پرپنہ ہو چھپائی رکھنی سی۔ کجّ چِرے توں بعد پنہ کی لگا ایہہ جنگل نی ناں اُسی جنگلی درندے بہڑنیں، جنّے ایہہ غل ہونی جنگلی درندے ہکے واری کھائی جان آں، مہاڑے جسّے نال مہاڑی رومے تے مغزے کی زاو نہ دین آں، پنہ نی سِس تے سہورا جِڑے پنہ نیں ابے صابرے تے اسئنی اماں کی آخنے سن اساں اسنکی بنائی تئی رکھسا ہن آخنے سن اساں نیں پترے ٹکی ولیت پہچانانی تے اُتھئی ڈنگراں نی پاہ سونی ہوئے آں۔

کہارے وچ رولا ٹغا رہنا سی جس نی واز آنڈیاں گمانڈیاں کی وی اشنّنی رہنی سی۔ پنہ نی ہک گماڈن سکھنی سی۔ ہک دیہارے باہر کھلتیاں آخیاس
پینو، تیرا مرد تینوں مار دا کٹدا ہے۔ اے ڈومیسٹک ابیوز ہے۔ توں پولیس نوں دس۔
پنہ اسنّے منویں اِل تکی پُچھیا
او کہہ ہونا ہے۔
سکھنی سمجھایا

جے توہاڈا آدمی توہانوں مارکٹ کر دا ہوئے تے تُسی پلس نوں دس سکدے ہو۔ پلس توہاڈے گھر آلے نوں نپ کے لے جاسی ۔ اُنہوں جیل وچ ڈک کے تینوں کھار وی دوائے گی تے پیسے وی۔

پینہ سکھنی آل تکی مسکڑی کیتی
میکی ڈومیسٹک ایبیوز ناں پتہ نئی۔ بس اتنا پتہ ھ جے پہیونی گلائی لج کہ راہ رکھی نی اس دیہاڑے راتی میکسی کھار مڑیا تے کج زیادہ ہی نشے وچ سی۔ پہلیں وی جہڑی چیز ہتھے آئی جائے ماری جاناں ہونا سی ۔ اج اسئے ہتھے لنگری کٹّے آلا مُولناں آئی گیا ۔ پہلیں پینہ نیں سرے فئرنگے تے موے چوں خون نکلیا۔ آخری ساہ تھوں پہلاں پینہ آخیا
ابا میں تُسانی گلائی لج رکھی ایہہ۔

(افتخار کلوال)

Honour

By Iftikhar Kahval

Pina was lost in her own world since the last few days. She stayed quiet but was always smiling like she had butterflies in her stomach. She always covered her face to smile quietly or bit her hand whilst shying away. Even though the leaves had fallen and trees dried up, Pina's face was fresh like the spring.

Recently her paternal aunt had asked Pinas dad for her hand in marriage for Farooq. These times were such where sons and daughters obeyed their parents' requests and wishes. Pina and Farooq had never spoke of this with each other, but they were both attracted to each other.

Pinas dad, Farooq's maternal uncle, Chaudhary Sabar was a well-known person. The whole village respected him. He was good at heart but was short-tempered. If he saw something bad happening, he often expressed his anger. Everyone knew, once Chaudhary Sabar says something it is final. Like everyone else, Farooq was also scared of his uncle.

Farooq and Pinas homes were close to each other, with a few fields in between. Farooq's mum, Nasreen, had only once spoken about Farooq and Pinas rishta. Pinas dad had not agreed straight away but said he would think about it. Yet, Pina was flying, she thought she was a fairy touching the clouds.

Pina was lost in these thoughts as she carried home water filled from the well. As she reached home, she saw Bawa Pajja's son and daughter-in-law sat there. They were from the next village but were settled in the UK. After saying "salam" Pina continued her house chores. As they left, Pina heard them saying "We will see you tomorrow, Lala". Pina thought they have visited today so what is the need for them to come again tomorrow.

She continued her work. Pina heard her parents whispering to each other. Pina's dad asked her younger sister Jina to go call her aunt Nasreen. Farooq's mum left all her housework and raced to her brother's house. On the way she thought to herself she should have brought something sweet rather than coming empty handed. Pina was kneading dough outside the kitchen. Farooq's mum took a deep breath as she thought Pina would soon light up her house by becoming Farooq's wife and that they will make a wonderful couple.

Choudry Sabar said "Sister, I have called you here to discuss something."

"Yes, tell me." Nasreen said excitedly, she was happy her brother wanted her opinion for the first time.

"Bawa Pajjas son and daughter-in-law came and they asked for Pinas rishta," said Chaudry Sabar.

Hearing this Nasreen couldn't hide the shock on her face. Pina's hands froze midway kneading the dough. She felt like her wings had been clipped and she had hit the hard floor.

Pina heard her father continuing "Bawa Pajja and our ancestors were the same, accepting this proposal will refresh old relations. Nasreen, I will give you my younger daughter's hand instead."

The next day Pinas Father promised her hand to Bawa Pajjas grandson. At night, Chaudhary Sabar saw a light shining outside his house. The light kept drifting away from the house and then back towards the house.

Chaudhary Sabar shouted out, "Who is it!". The light switched off and you could hear footsteps running away.

Farooq could not build the confidence to say it to his uncle himself, so he went home and told his mum. The next day Farooq's mum went to Chaudhary Sabar's house and started crying. She was scared of her brother and that made her cry. Chaudry Sabar and his wife asked Nasreen what's wrong.

After some time, she built the courage and started to speak, "My Farooq said, don't marry Pina to Bawa Pajjas grandson. He is not a good person, he has already been married once and everyone says he is drug addict."

Nasreen started crying again, "Farooq says its ok if uncle doesn't want me to marry Pina but please don't get her married to a man who will ruin her life."

Everyone went quiet. The silence was deafening.

Finally, Chaudhary Sabar spoke, "Everyone knows whatever Sabar says happens, he does not go back on his word."

As he sat his daughter in the bridal palanquin, Chaudry Sabar said to her, "Putar, when a daughter marries into a house, she only leaves it at her funeral. Please respect your father's honour."

Manan, who was nicknamed Maxi, had one silver tooth. He was dark skinned, had a big nose and bloodshot read eyes. He wore a thick silver chain around his neck and a piercing in one ear. Pina's heart filled with fear as she saw Manan for the first time.
Pina came to the UK. The UK was like a jungle surrounded by water, filled with horrid animals who abused Pina. Pina had scratches across her face and burn marks on her arms, but she tried her best to hide these. After some time, Pina realised it's not a jungle, else the animals would have finished her in one go. But Pina was not only physically abused she was abused mentally and emotionally too. Her soul was hurting.

Pina's father-in-law and mother-in-law, who promised her father they would treat her like their own daughter, now said, "Our son brought you to the UK, otherwise you would have been cleaning animal shit in your village." This abuse had become a regular occurrence. The neighbours would also hear the things Pina suffered.

One day a Sikh lady, who was one of Pina's neighbours, said to her "Pina, your husband beats you. This is domestic abuse. You should tell the police."

Pina asked, "What is that?"

The Sikh lady explained, "If your partner physically hits you, you can tell the police. They will arrest him. The police will also help house you and you can get your own money."

Pina smiled at the Sikh lady, "I don't know about domestic abuse. I just know how to uphold my father's honour."

That same night Maxi returned home highly intoxicated. He would normally grab the first thing he found and beat Pina. Today, he found the pestle. Pina started bleeding from her head, then from her nose and mouth. In her last breath she said "Father, I honoured your word."

Sin

کڑیاں اک گناہ

Nabeela Ahmed

تیناں ناں پیدا ہونا ہی گناہ اے
اساں پنوں مٹھائی بنڈ ڈآں
یا بکرے دیاں نیاز
دلی خوشی اساں کی
پترے نال ہی ہونی اے

پرآواں پہنناں شرٹاں لائیاں تہ کہہ ہویا؟
سردی آلا ملکھ اے، اتھے جنہے اسہے طرح لائین
فر سکولے ناں یونیفارم وی اے
جے پہناں لائی پینٹ، یا ڈریس تہ ٹائیٹ
تہ شرمے نال مرن نغے ماپیؤ
تہ بے عزت ہوئی گیا خاندان
انہاں کی شلوار قمیض پیری تہ پیچو
ناں انہاں کی سردی لگنی اے
تہ ناگوریاں نے طعنے تہ محول
او کہار وی چلسن، تہ بار وی

جے مڑ ہے رکھی گرلفریندڈ کہار آیا لیٹ
تم رہے کرنے ہونین نا اے کم
جے کڑی کی آئی گیا کوئی پسند
یا مڑی کتھوں لیٹ
تہ عزت مٹی چ ملی گئی سارے کنبے نی
او اک بچ ہ نا ہوئی، ململھے نا چنڈا ہوئی

او اپنے جمن ہونے نے گناہ نا کفارا کرسی

ہر جغہ، ہر روز
مائو پیسو نے ہر کم سنحی تہ
اپنی ہر خواہش کی ماری تہ
انہاں نی مرضی پر چلی تہ
جتھے سٹن انہاں کی قبول کری تہ

ساوریاں نے ناں وچ شاہد انسیکیوریٹی تہ کنٹرول اے
ہک زندگی لائی تہ کڑہی اپنی جغہ بنا سی
جہیری کدہے وی اسنی پکی نی ہوئی
ترہہ لفظ، تہ جنہان نی تسّاں خدمتاں کتیاں زاراں
انہاں او الزام لانے، جھ تسّاں کی اپنی انہاں نال
ہر نیکی پر افسوس ہوسی

گنہگار جنانی اللہ ہونی پاک تہ لائق عبادت
چلہے بنئی ماہ، او وہ بڈھیری عمر اوچ
فر جنت اسنے پیراں تھلے
اس تھوں پہلے اسی دینا پینا ہر پل ثبوت
ہر غلطی، ہر خامی نے پچھے آخر او ہی جے اے

ربا ماریا، توں کہہ لخیا قرآن وچ؟
اساں کی بنانا ہی گناہ سی
تہ نا بنائیں آہ
جمنے توں مرنے تک نی نفرت تہ شکاں
کولوں اساں تھکی گئیاں
ہن توں پلیز کڑیاں بناناں بند کر دی شور

Girls a Sin

Being born as a girl is a sin itself.
Despite giving mithai and niaz,
The true joy of our parents—
Is only if we are sons.

What does it matter if brothers wear trousers and shirts?
It's cold here—everyone wears them.
Even school has a uniform.
But if a girl wears trousers or a dress with tights
Her parents will die of shame,
And the whole family will be dishonoured.
Put her in a shalwar kameez,
She won't feel cold,
Nor the mocking of her peers.

She will bear at home and outside.
If a boy has a girlfriend or comes home late,
It's just a small mistake.
But if a girl likes someone or comes home late,
The family's honour is buried in the dirt.
Not like she is a child too, but rather a flag of nation

She must atone for the sin of being born—
Everywhere, every day.
Learn all the skills at her parents,
Kill every dream, send her wherever they deem fit.

Insecurity and control seem to be ingrained
In the name in-law
A girl struggles her whole life to find her place,

A place that is never truly hers.
Three words—"of tallaaq"—
Erase every sacrifice she ever made.
And the same people she served her whole life
Will accuse her of everything under the moon.

All women seen as sinful
Suddenly become pure and worthy of worship
when they become mothers, but only in old age!
Then heaven is beneath her feet.

Until then, every step she takes
Must be proof of her virtue.
Afterall, behind every mistake and every flaw,
She alone is to blame.

Oh God, tell me—
What did you write in the Quran?
If our very existence is a sin
Then you shouldn't have created us.
We are exhausted from birth to death,
From the hatred and suspicion that follows us.
Please, just stop making girls.

گناہ

Abdul Karim

سب تھوں پہلا گناہ اِبلیس کیتا
جیہڑے اُس آدم کی سجدہ نیئں کیتا
اس اپنے رب کی اتنا خفٰے کیتا
اللہ اسکی اپنے کولوں دفع کیتا
اس جانیاں جانیاں منگی کندھی اجازت مالک اصل کولوں
قیامت جیہاں میں گناہ کرواساں آدم نی سب نسل کولوں
سب توں پہلیں اس جائی تے آدم تے حوا کی برغلایا
اللہ نی نافرمانی کروائی تے انہاں کی جنت چوں کڈوایا
آدم پچھتایا یا می کی کیاں پنہل لگی گئی
شیطان خوش ہویا کہ ہون کُھل لبی گئی
فر اس ہابیل کی اپنے پہائی قابیل نے ہتھوں مروایا
مآڑیاں سوچاں اسنے دِلے وچ پاہی تے اپنا کم کروایا
شیطان تے شطونگڑے فر پوری دنیا وچ چھائی گئے
آدم نی آل آدی اللہ تھوں ہٹائی تے آپے نال لائی گئے
اللہ دسیا کہ رہ بچو انہاں کولوں پڑھی تے سورت النّاس
نی تاں انہاں نیاں گلاں بُجھی تے کر سو ستیا ناس

- 84 -

Sin

When Satan refused to prostrate to Adam, he committed the first sin,
He declared himself superior to Adam, being a haughtily arrogant Jinn.
His stubborn denial of divine command invoked the Almighty's ire,
Who expelled him from His company and condemned him to hellfire.

For his past service he sought from Allah just one permission,
When granted, he made misguiding humans his life's mission.
First, he went to Adam and Eve and made them ignore divine decree,
Inciting temptation, he made them eat the fruit of the Forbidden tree.

Adam was remorseful of committing sin,
Whilst Satan was celebrating his first win.
Next, he approached Adam's son Cain,
And got him to kill his brother in vain.

Satan and his cronies soon spread throughout the land,
Corrupting and misguiding humans with his evil band.
But if you read Sura An'Naas to seek Allah's protection,
You may be saved from Satan leading you to transgression.

Insan Banay Khuda

Kausar Mukhtar

Esaih aakhnayn hamal giranah gunnah eh
Musalmaan aakhnayn suud khana gunnah eh
Yahudi aakhnayn Waaray, dunyavi kam gunnah eh
Hindu aakhnayn motaa ghost khana gunnah eh
Saaray aakhayn arr gunnah ni mauth sazaah eh
Sazaah daynay vich baraa mazaah eh

Humans Playing God

Christians say abortion is sin
Muslims say consuming interest is sin
Jews say worldly work on the Sabbath is sin
Hindus say eating beef is sin
They all a concur the punishment for every sin should be death or something equally grim
They all relish in meting out punishment, I guess that's a win

امی نے رحم وچ

Farah Nazir

امی نے رحم وچ
فرشتہ آیا۔
نکھ ماری تے
میری دنیا نا راستہ تے رشتہ
کُھلی گیاں
شیطان نے وسوس
تے نفس نے وسوس
لوگاں نے وسوس۔
ماری دنیا نی کتاب کھلی
گئی
فرشتہ لکھنا سزا تے گا بے
پاسے۔
اندرنی دنیا
برائے نی دنیا
ماری نیت چنگی اے
ماری نیت چنگی اے
پر ماری دل تے دماغ نی لڑے۔
سجے نی سڑک باری
اوکھی

شیطان نے وسوس
تے نفس نے وسوس
تے لوگاں نے وسوس
ماری نیت چنگی اے
پر دنیا نی چمک وی چنگی۔
ڈورن تے پراناں آہ
مروہ تے صفا طرف۔
اگے نا چھے
لوگ ماری خدا بن گئے ان
گناں نے مطلب وی گئے
گناں نے مطلب وی گئے
ای نہ کر
نہ کریا
نہ کریا
نہ کریا
گناں نے مطلب وی گئ
فنائ فِ اللہ
، فنائ فِ اللہ کِہ را اچھا اے
آزادی توں بغیر۔
موت نا فرشتہ روز آچنا
فنائ فِ اللہ اے سی
حی، حی، حی

Ammi ne Rahm Vich

Farah Nazir

Ammi ne rahm vich,
Frista aya.
Pookh mari teh,
Mari dunya na rasta teh rishta
Kuli gayan.

Shaitan ne waswaas,
Teh nafs ne waswaas,
Loga ne waswaas.

Mari dunya ni kitab kuli gi—
Frishta likhna saja teh gabe paseh.
Andar ni dunya,
Baray ni dunya.

Mari Niyat Changi Eh
Mari niyat changi eh,
Bur mara dil the damkh ni laray
eh.
Sajay ni sarkh bari okhi—
Shaitan ne waswaas,
Teh nafs ne waswaas,
Teh loga ne waswaas.

Mari niyat changi eh,
Bur dunya ni chamkh vi changi.
Dornay teh pirnay ae,
Marwa teh safa taraf.

Ageh na pichay,
Log maray khuda banigay an.

Ghunay ne Matlab Vi Gay

Ghunay ne matlab vi gay—
Ay na kar,
Na karya,
Na karya,
Na karya.
Ghunay ne matlab vi gay.

Fanafilla

Fanafilla kisra acha eh,
Azaadi tu bagair.
Mowt na fristha roz achna,
Fanafilla ay si—
Hayy Hayy Hayy.

The Womb of My Mother

The womb of my mother,
The angel came,
Blew into me.
The paths and bonds of this
world
Opened wide.

The devil whispers,
The ego whispers,
The people whisper.

The book of my world
opened—
The angels write on the left
and right.
My inner world,
My outer world.

My intention is good,
My intention is good,
But my heart and mind are at
war.
The right path is hard.

The devil whispers,
The ego whispers,
The people whisper.

My intention is good,
But the sparkles of the world
shine good too.
Running here, running there,
From Marwa to Safa,
Neither ahead nor behind.
People have become my god.

The meaning of misdeeds is
lost,
The meaning of wrongdoing is
gone.

Don't do this,
Don't do it,
Don't do it,
Don't do it,
Don't do it.

The meaning of pain is lost.

Fanafilla
How will Fanafilla come
Without freedom?
The angel of death visits
every day.
Fanafilla will come—
Hayy, Hayy, Hayy.

Gunah

Awais Hussain

گُناہ
گُناہ اِک گُون اے ظالم
بندیاں کی برے تے مری سکنے
یا گُناہ اِک چیز اے چمُوٹنے آلی
بندے ڈاہڈے پھسنے

جے گُناہ نال بندے پلیت اوئی جانے
فِر اساں سارے گندگی نال بھرے وئے آں
سمندراں چ اِتنا پانی کوئی دھونے واسطے
فِر اِس مہیل کی کسطرح کڈاں

اپنیاں دِلاں کی صاف کرو
سچائی نے سبُوں نال مارو
پیار نے اپانی نال سیرو
تے پڑی پر رکھی تے
چنگے طریقے نال ملَو

تے ڈمنی نال مارو
کیاں جے گُناہ کرنے تھیں بعد
کُٹ تے پہینی اِ ہی پہینی اے

مارو چار واری پنج واری
جتنی دیر لغنی مہیل لہنے واسطے
سارا مہیل کڈو
تے تارو
بالٹی چ ڈبوئی تے
تے تاری تے
نچوری تے کھلہیرو

کوشش کرو کہ اَگلی واری داغ نہ لگے
بہوں مُشکل نال لہیے نیں ن
پر جے گُناواں تھیں نی بچن اونا
تے دھونے نی جاچ سِکھی گھنو

Gunah

Gunah ik gūn eh zālim
Bandeyañ ki bireh teh mari sakne
Ya gunah ik cheez eh chamūtne aly
Bande ḍāḍeh phasne

Jey guna naal bandy paleet uwi jaaney
fir asañ saarey gandgi naal bhary vey añ
Samundrañch itna pāṇi koni dhone vasteh
Fir is mehl ki kistra kaḍañ

Apnyañ dilāñ ki sāf karo
Sachai ne saboon nāl māro
Pyār ne pāṇi nāl sero
Teh paṛi par rakhi teh
Changy tareeqy nāl malloh

Teh ḍamni nāl māro
Kiyañ jeh gunah karney thiñ bād
Kuṭṭ teh peyni hi peyni eh

Māro chār vāri panj vāri
Jitni der lagni mehl lene vasteh
Sāra mehl kaḍo
Teh tāro
Baḷtich ḍabuwi teh
Te tāri teh
Nachōri teh khlero

Koshish karo k aghli vāri dagh na lageh
Bouñ mushkil nāl lenen
Par jey gunāvañ thīñ ni bachan ona
Fir dhone ni jāch sikhi ghin

Sin

Sin is a viper, cruel,
If it bites, a person can die.
Or a snare that clings and sticks,
Trapping people badly.

If with sin, people become unclean,
Then we are all filled with dirt.
There is not enough water in the oceans to wash it,
So how can we remove this filth?

Clean your hearts.
Scrub it with the soap of truth,
Soak it with the water of love,
Place it on a stone,
And rub it well.

Beat it with a stick,
For after sin, pain is inevitable.

Strike it four or five times,
Or as long as it takes to remove the dirt.
Remove all the filth.
And wash it clean. Not sure your need this stanza, but I liked the use of old words in Pahari, so had left it

Dip it in a bucket,
Wash it,
Rinse it, and hang it to dry.
Try to avoid staining it again,

For stains are difficult to remove.
But if you cannot spare yourself from sin,
Learn how to cleanse it.

Sazaa

Nafisa Akhtar

Mey har insaan ar kaafi guna kitheyn,
Mey har banday ar kaafi maafiyaan mangian

Guna ik kamini chiz eh, beymari ar astha khai jana dil-khuda nal bewafai
Kithna Rabb raheem eh, bachana eh, kay na pohncheh asaki koi tabai

Akhar insaan ah, pulna sara kam eh
Kithna Rabb kareem eh, asa duay ney guna thaki teh, akhnay ah "kithna beysharm eh?"

Sharmindgi teh haali hath nal, Khuda ni bakhshish mangnay ah
Key burray lokan ni aadatan saray par rang na charri jaan

Kapray saaf sutray laanay ahn, par dil rehnay mehlay
Apnay nal larna pehna
Gustakiyan nay samundar tarna pehna

Guna ik moka eh
Khuda kol kharna eh ya door satna eh

Punishment

Just like others, I have many sins
Just like others, I too have asked forgiveness

Sin is shrewd, like a virus slowly eating away at you —
disloyal to its host

How compassionate is the Lord, He saves us from ruin
After all, to be human is to forget

How generous is the Lord, He gives to us even when we
look upon others' mistakes, saying "are they not
ashamed?"

With shy, empty palms we ask in penance
That by the sinners' company, we are not spoiled

Our appearance may be clean yet our hearts are soiled
In order to fight our egos, we must swim in the seas of
disobedience

You see, sin is an opportunity; where God draws us nearer
or casts us further away from Him

Love Letters to Our Past and Future

Abba Ji

Nafisa Akhtar

May pehley kadeh khat ni likhya, thussa ar miki zyada gaanay sunanay, teh sheyr shayri ni aadat payi gi si. So mara pehla khat apni zuban vich thusanki likhni ah.

Thusa nay begher zindgi kaafi badli gi eh, par thusan ni naseeatan mey kadeh na pulni.

Akhney ohnay so kay "look" "listen" "speak" karya kar. Thaki na kun bolna? Keh akhya nay? Teh fir apni rai teh jawab dey na, bass thu sirf speak karri jani ey!

"Jeyra kuj dilleh vich chupanay oh, baar zahir karya karo;" iski 'table talk' bulaanay so.

"Changay sohnay kapray lau, teh saaf sutray boot, fir apni respect barni eh," mey kadeh ni thakya banda itna shawq rakhna, thussa ar, apni surat vich. Kalf lana, baal ki set rakhna, kangi apne gojay vich, ramaal kaprey ni, naal rakhi vi, teh boot har veyley polish hoi vey. Asa ki keh patha si? sohnay dillan alay, Allah nay sohnay banday, har haalat vich sohnay lagnayn.

Thusan miki dasya key naseeat ki, qabooliyat chaynieh, waseeat ki hikmat chaynieh. Agley naslan ki keh das-so, jey pichleyan nay kahaniyan pulso? Bachay mustaqbal ni umeedan nay, zindgi ni roshni ni kiran an.

Thusaniyan mehnatan teh thussaniya qurbaniyan, daleyri teh himmat nal itheh aye soh teh navi zindgi banaee.

Kay kehi? vaari miki lagna key thusa thu begheyr; thusaniya gallan, honsla, teh pyaar thu begher may rayi na sakni. Fir har chiz disni, thusani awaaz achsi; gussayvich ya laad nal, maray naal rehnay oh.

Pyo nay lafzan ik chath teh dewaar ar ohnayn- mazbooth sardiyan thu bachana, garmiyan vich sukoon deyneyn teh baarshan kulu aman.

Shukr eh key thussa miki ay gallan bayyan,
fir may agleyan ki ba'e sakni ah ke ay naseeatan thusan dasiyyan.

Allah ni hifazat teh karam vich ryo... agley jahaan vich milsa

Thussa ni nikki thee
x

Letter to a Loved one

Dear Dad,

I've never written a letter before. Like you, I prefer listening to songs, and reading poetry. So, my first letter in my own language, I will write to you.

Without you, life has changed so much, but your advices I'll never forget.

You used to say "look, listen, then speak" You look at whose talking, what are they saying? Then you respond with your own opinion, but you just keep talking!" "Say it out loud, whatever you hide in your hearts" you'd call that "table talk."

"Wear good quality beautiful clothes, and clean shoes to be respectable" I've never seen a person who paid so much attention to their appearance. Dyed hair, neatly styled with a pocket comb, that you carried with you, as well as cloth handkerchief and well- polished shoes. How were we to know, that kind hearted beautiful people, God's own people, are always beautiful in all their states?

You once told me that, "advice needs a willing acceptance, counsel needs wisdom. What will you teach the coming generations, if you'll forget the stories of our forefathers? Children are the hope of the future, and the rays of light of our lives."

It's because of your efforts and sacrifices, your courage and motive that bought you here, to make a new life.

At times I feel that, without you, without your words, consolation, encouragement and love, I cannot live. Then I see it all, I hear your voice, in anger or affection- you are always with me.

A father's words are like a sheltering house – strong. Weathering the cold winters, and cooling in the summer's heat, shielding us from the rain. Thank God you shared these wisdoms with me, a means for me to share them with our children, timeless advices that'll stay with us forever.

In God's protection I leave you...and will meet you again in the next abode.

Your youngest
X

ماریاں بڑیاں تہ بچیاں نے ناں اک خط

Nabeela Ahmed

تسآں سہولت واسطے اپنیاں بچیاں
کی بچپن وچ چجیا سی پردیس
کدے مرہی بہرے پڑھن نی سن ہوئے
کوئی نہ کوئی ولائیت ہونا سی
کہاڑ لینٹر تہ ہوئی گے دپر رہے خالی

امی ابو، تسآں مائو، پیو نی واز سجھے بغیر مدتاں گزاریاں
پر آئے ململکھے چ ہر اپنے ململکھے نے کی اپنیاں آر تکیا
ڈاڈ، تسآں رقعے لنخے، لفظاں وتیاں
اپنے نکھے مکانے چ بہوں آں کی چھت دیتی
مم، تسآں جسنے وی ماہ پیو نا اتھے وہین
اسنی مائو نی جغہ کیندی، اسنے بچیاں نے نھیال نی
تسآں نے جنازے پر او ساریاں تیاں آئیاں سن
اپنی مائو کی اخری واری شکریہ آخنے واسطے
بچیاں قرآن دتے سن، اپنی نانی تہ

تساں نے پوتر دو ہتر یاد رکھنین کہ کس نی بنیاد اھن
تہ روکی کہنین اپنے آپ کی، تساں نی بدنامی نہ وہے

- 104 -

تسّاں نی مشکلاں انہاں کی اسطرح لغنیاں
جسطرح کتابی کہانیاں وہین، یا میوزیم وچ رکھی آں چیزآں

تسّاں نا کہاڑ انہاں تے خولیڈے خوم اے
چلے افورڈ کری سکن ، اھ تسّاں وی سمجھنے سو

جہیڑا انہاں نا کہاڑ اے، اوھ انہاں کی تکی آخنین پڑائے لوک
تسّاں نے ملکھے نے لوک، یا انہاں کی کرنین استعمال
یا انہاں کی آخنین غلط، ایھ کدھے سمجھنے نی انہاں کی
کدھے بہنووں زیادہ سمجھی جانین

گورے انہاں کی باقی اخنین
تہ پاکستانی انہاں کی ولائیتی

A Letter for My Elders and Youngsters

Nabeela Ahmed

You sent your children away in their childhood,
For the sake of ease, for a better tomorrow.
Courtyards never truly filled again
Someone was always in England
Houses turned into concrete structures,
Yet remained empty.

Mum, dad—
You spent your years without hearing the voices of your parents.
In a foreign land, you treated everyone from home
As your own
Dad, you wrote letter for others, gave them lifts
In your tiny house you provided a roof for many
Mum, whoever didn't have parents here
You offered them a parent's home
Their children a nanhyaal
All those daughters came mum, to your funeral
To say thanks for the final time
The children offered Quran-e-Paak for their Nani

Your grandchildren remember their roots, you
And restrain themselves, so that you would never feel embarrassed.
Your struggles seem to them like fairy tales,
Or like preserved artifacts in a museum.

Your home is a holiday home for them,
Only when they could afford to visit.
You, understood this.
The people of your homeland
Either use them or judge them.
The youngsters either don't understand them
Or understand them far too well.

The English call them Paki,
And the Pakistanis call them foreigners.

Sareh Grahn ni Cheejah

Nafeesa Hamid

Sareh grahn ni cheejah
Kiri keri cheej chai niyah? je kohni teeka, khaar a
meh ahni deh sa, koi dar-fikar ni bacheh
satharaahn saalaha si yehn? meh saarya ni look after
khaar a - Aftabs nyoh schoola neh kapreh
kiri cheej chai neh? eh loh das pound, das pound aur
bachyah theh: shirt, trousers, skirt, blazer, swimming
bivi thehn – batweh, sohneh niya chaapah bangah
khaar a - shaadi ay gi? Acho acho shaadiyahn ni seerth tha
unseerth kaprayahn nya dakaana, kuseh nya shaapah
khaar a - next door Pal Pharmacy thu Charlie ni spray
kiri cheej chayni neh? Veet, perfume, clips, bobbles
khaar a - town kiya jasoh? Hair bands, t shirt'ah dressah

town nah ka faida jeh Alum Rock thu yeh labi jasi?
Ka cheej chai ni? sab koch labi jaana, sab koch khaar a
sabzi frruit gosht chooza machi doodh andeh pyaaz
khaar a, kah lori naya bacho? shapahn aaleh pochneh
khaar a - thosah asah ki bao, asahn ahni desahn

What You Can Get in Our Village

What is it you need? Don't worry, it's all good
I got you, don't fret or fear my beloved child
Haven't I looked after everyone since I was 17?
It's all good – school uniform's straight from Aftab's
What is it you need? It's all good
Here's £10, take £10 more
For my children – shirts, trousers, skirts, blazers, swim
For my wife – purses, gold rings, gold bangles
It's all good, don't fret – weddings coming up?
Come come, we've got stitched and unstitched cloth
Kuseh shoe shops, it's all good don't fret or fear
Next door is Pal pharmacy if you need Veet or Charlie
Tell me what you need – is it perfumes, clips, bobbles
It's all good, no need to ever go to town – I got you
Hair bands, t-shirts, dresses – what's town got

What can you find there that you can't find in Alum Rock?
What is it you need? I'll find you anything you want
Don't fret, it's all good – veg, fruit, meat, chicken, fish
Eggs, milk, bread and onions
It's all good and blessed, what you need? Shop uncles ask
It's all good, tell us what you need, we'll find and bring to you

Romantic Love

Eh din nava Nakor

Imran Hafeez

ماڑے والد صاحب نا اک کلام تح ماڑا انگریزی ترجمہ

ایہہ دن نواں نکور
کل کیہہ ہویا
کل کیہہ ہوسی
نہ کر اس تے غور
ایہہ دن نواں نکور او سجناں ایہہ دن نواں نکور
ٹہپ چمکیلی لبھی پھرنی
تہارے جیہا کوئی اور او سجناں
ایہہ دن نواں نکور
چٹے پہڑ نیلے اسمانے
ٹرنے توہاڑی ٹوہر او سجناں
ایہہ دن نواں نکور
باغاں وچ پُھل رنگ برنگے
خشبویاں ناں زور او سجناں
ایہہ دن نواں نکور

سوو ے نرم گلاباں اپر
مکھیاری ناں شور او سجناں
ایہہ دن نواں نکور
برف ڈھلی پر اوہ نئیں آیا
جس ہتھ مہاڑے ڈور او سجناں
ایہہ دن نواں نکور
کدے نیں نکنے کم دنیا نے
کڈھ دلے چوں غم دنیا نے
کدے تے مہاڑے کوئی بہی تے
سن سدراں ناں شور او سجناں
ایہہ دن نواں نکور

حفیظ جوہر

(Translation of Hafeez Johar's poem 'Eh din nava Nakor') It's a brand-new day

What happened yesterday and what will tomorrow,
No need to dwell…
It's a brand-new day my dearest, today is brand-new.

The sunshine calls me towards you…
It's a brand-new day my dearest, today is brand-new.

The white clouds on blue sky canvas move as you do…
It's a brand-new day my dearest, today is brand-new.

A garden of colourful flowers and the strength of scent…
It's a brand-new day my dearest, today is brand-new.

The buzzing bee on a velvet red rose…
It's a brand-new day my dearest, today is brand-new.

The worldly affairs will never stop,
So, drop the worries from your heart.
Come and sit with me sometime,
And let's listen to the sounds of the soul…

It's a brand-new day my dearest, today is brand-new.

لولینگوج

Nabeela Ahmed

مہاڑی تہ اسنی لولینگوج بھگی اے
میں لفظاں نی تاجر آں
مارا سارا خزآنہ چند حرف ان

اسکی لفظاں نال چڑ اے
لفظ بولنے آلے اسکی چوٹھے لغنین
اسنی کرنسی عمل ان، صرف عمل
او مہاری تعریف نی کری سکناں
او اسکی مسکا لغنا اے
پر جلہے میں تیار ہوئی تے
پہریاں پڑوں ٹلہآں
تہ ہتھ کھلتا آ
بت بنی تہ کی تکنا اے

ہے میں کراں شکایت کہ ہے چیز کوئی نی کہار
تہ اسہے اہلے، جائی تے دو کنی آہنا اے
جہیڑی میں منگاں چیز
او ہک ہک کڑہی تہ پوری کرنا اے

اپنے شوق پہلائی تَں
ماہری ہر خواہش پوری کرنا اے

پرجے میں منگے دو لفظ پیار نے
تَہ گہیںنا پڑسی ماہرے نال

میں ہک ڈکشنری بنائی اے
او عملاں کی حرفاں وچ کنورٹ کرنی اے
ہن او چلہے ار لگرے نے چار ڈبے کہاڑ آنے
میں پڑھنی آں
اے کی چنگی لغنی اے
اسکی اے چاہ پسند اے

چلہے او ماری گڈی ناں تیل پانی چیک کرہے
مارے کہے ٹرپے تھوں پہلے
میں تکنی آں لکے آ
اسکی کج ہوئی نا جاے
میں کہہ کرساں

مہاڑی تَں اسنی لو لینگوج بھگلی اے

Love Language

Mine and his love language is different.
I am a trader of words,
My entire wealth is just a few letters.

He hates words
He sees those who say things as liars
His currency is actions, just actions
He can't compliment me
He sees it as buttering up
But when I get ready
And come down the stairs
He stands at the bottom
Staring at me like a statue

If I ever complain, we don't have this
He will immediately go and buy two
Whatever I ask for
He gets one by one
Forgetting his own desires
He fulfils my every wish

But if I ask for two words of love
He will fight with me for an hour

I have made a dictionary
It converts actions into words
Now, when he brings four boxes
Of Earl Grey home
I read it as:
'I like her and she likes this tea'

When he checks the oil and water in my car
Before one of my trips
I see written:
'If something happens to her
What will I do?'

Mine and his love language is different.

جوری نی جور

Farah Nazir

جہڑا پانیاں نا سمندر
جُڑنا اے
اک اور
سمندر نال،
او اکھی سمندر بن جانے
آن
اکھی سمندر۔
او اکھی سمندر بنی جانے
آن
اکھی سمندر۔
اسرا ساریہ جوری بنی
آن
اسرا ساری جوری بنی
اے۔
پتا نی لگ آہ
آستے آستے جُڑ بنی اے
جہڑا دو سمندر
جُڑنے آن

ہالی اُنہاں کی پتا لگ نا اے
کتو آیا
کتو شروع ہویا
کتو ختم ہویا۔
جہرا اک لہر دوّی لہر
نال
جُڑنا
پتا نی لگنا
، تے
دوّی لہر کتو شروع ہوئی
اے۔
اس طرح ساریا جوڑی
بنی آن۔
اس طرح ساری کہانیاں
لکھن اوئیاں
اکھی
اکھی بنی گئی اے۔
لاڈا نا سمندر وچ
تکلیفاں تے درد
ڈبی جانیاں۔
پیرا توں جڑ لکھنیاں
دل توں روپ لکھنا

تے منڈے پُر پچھلے پار تینے
آں۔
جیا
لگی اصلی تنخیاس
لگی اصلی تنخیاس
بردہ توں بغیر۔
ماری اندرلی دنیا
تے ان
او گواہ دینا
ماری بارے نی دنیا۔
لاڈا نا سمندر وچ
میں آزادی آں۔
،دنیا نی چمک
دسی پئے آں۔
مارے اپنی چمک
دسی پئے آں۔

Jori ni Jor

Jisra panya-na samondar,
Jurna eh ik aur samondar naal,
O ikhi samondar bani jaanay an—
Ikhi samondar.
Isra saaria jori bani an,
Isra sari jori bani eh.
Pata ni lag ah, Astaay astaay jor
bani eh
Jisra do samondar
Jur nay an
Hali unaki pata lag na eh
Kutu aya,
Kutu shuru oya,
Kutu khatam oya.
Jisra ik lahr dooi lahr nai naal,
Jurna,
Pata ni lagna
Kutu ik lahr shuru oi ya,
Teh,
Dooah lahr kutu shuru oi ya.
Is tarah saria jori bani an.
Is tarah saari kahaniya likhin oi
yan,
Ikhi,
Ikhi bani gay ah.
Laada na samondar vich,
Takleefa te dard,
Dobi janyan.
Paira to jarr likhnayan,
Dil tu roop likhna,

Teh munday puru pichlay paar
tanayan.
Jiya,
Miki asli takhyas,
Miki asli takhyas,
Barda to bagair.
Mari andar ni duniya,
Teh un,
o gawaah dena
Mari baaray ni duniya.
Laada na samondar vich,
Mai azadi ah.
Duniya ni chamak,
Dasi painay an
Maray apne chamak,
Dasi painay an.

The Strength of Union

Like the waters of the ocean,
Merging with another ocean,
It becomes one ocean—
One single ocean.
This is how all unions are formed,
This is how our union was formed.
Without realising,
It began slowly, their bond,
When two oceans meet.
Only they know.
When it began,
When it started,
When it ended.
Like one wave meeting the next—
Joining,
Without knowing
When one began,
And when the other followed.
This is how all unions are made.
This is how our story was written,
One by one,
Becoming one.
In the ocean of love,
Pain and sorrow drown.
Roots come out from the feet,
Light emerges from the heart,
And ancient weight falls off
From the shoulders.
Because,
they saw my true reflection,

they saw me —
Without a veil.
My inner world,
And they bear witness
To my outer world.
In the ocean of love,
I am free.
The light of the world,
She speaks to me.
My own light,
She speaks to me.

Pyar ka Mausam

Kausar Mukhtar

Sardiyah wich changa langa weh jilleh twaaray haatha nhi
garmi mareh tandyaa hatha kih pakhani eh
Garmiyah wich daryaah nay kinaray
sair karnah, darkhtaa
nay taleh kalloy keh jappi panaa
Suweh, Peelay, Ghulabi rang phullaN nay
Allah sajaa-eeh dunya beshumar sohnayaa nazaarehya
naal
Badaami aakha, saawalah rang, kaaleh, kungraleh baal
Koy sheh ni milni mikki tawarehya
nakhshehya naal

Season of Love

On winter mornings the warmth of your hands holding
mine
feels like a gentle fire
Summer walks besides rivers hand in hand holding each
other
close beneath the shade of trees
Red, yellow, pink, flowers vibrant in endless shades of
colour
endless colour, God has decorated the world with
immeasurable
beauty
Your hazel eyes, dark skin, wavy black hair
Nothing holds my gaze as much as your sight

Pyar aur Waqt

Kausar Mukhtar

Jjilleh tusah kol ohnay oh waqt chorah naluh tayz nasnaa eh
Dur ohneh oh teh raseeh ni ghandeh akh dilleh ki kasnaa eh

Love and Time

When we are together time runs faster than a thief
When apart time tightens like a knot tied around my heart
Each moment slow, painful and full of grief

Doh tuh Ik

Tuh atta the meh paani
Tari fitrat wich khushki
Mari tabiyat wich rawani
Jilleh paysi mukkiyaa ni maar
Atta ja-ee keh ohsee tyar

2 become 1

You're flour & I'm water
Your nature is dry
Whereas I like to flow
A good kneading is necessary
To turn us in to dough

میں نظم لوڑنے تھیں گیا ساں

Abdul Raouf Qureshi

میں نظم لوڑنے تھیں گیا ساں
نیرے وچ چھچنا
سردیاں نی شامیں
کفتاں تھوں پہلیں
چن نی سی چڑیا اجے سویل سی
لوکی منجی ڈنگر
ڈکنے پے سے
ککڑاں بکریاں نی واز ا چھے

پیڑھے اپر چڑھنا
پلبارے کی ترپنا
کنڈیاں نال پلپچنا
میں نکے اپر جائ کھلتاں

دور میرپور شہرے نیاں لیٹاں دسن
لینڈ سے پاسے جہازاں نیاں بتیاں

شیداں لائنیاں
نیرے وچ ٹولنیاں
چیکڑے وچ تلکنیاں

باڑیاں وچ کھوبنیاں
ماڑی اکھیں او کہار لوڑی کیندا
جیتے توتے نا بوٹا سی
پیڑھے وچ جھنڈ
جھنڈی ہٹ لیل

میں نکا جیا ساں موکڑی ار
جیلے لوخ چھی
لیت پچھی
میکی کونی سی پتا اس 'دردے' نا کہہ ناں اے

وقت گزر نا ریا
میں لیلے نا بیر بنتا تکیا
بیرے اپر چڑھنا رنگ
میں تکیا
اسکی پیلا ھونا
نیلی تاری نی جڑے ار
کنڈل ماریاں

ماڑا دل کرے ہتھ لانس
خشبو سینگھاں
کول بالاں
ڈراں کوڑا بولیا جے

- 128 -

سوچیا آئی لو یو آخاں
دلے اچ آئی
جے جوتی لائی کیندیس

ویلا لنگنا ریا
دیر ہوئی گی
میں جھنڈی کی سوا ہونا تکیا
بیری کی پکنا
کاں ڈارنے شیشے
ماڑی انکھیں
انیاں گیتاں
کئیں واریں طوطے میں ڈارے

وقت ٹرنا ریا

میں بھجیا
کنبل پھولی سی
اس پیلے کپڑے لائے سے
کیلی اپر پھل جمیا
بھوئی ارد سمنی سی
سوہنے آلا روپ سمیس
کھجورے آلا نخرہ
عطر گلاباں سٹے سے

خشبو میں تک پوچی سی
میں بھجیا
تو سی ٹو لکی بجائ اے
رو ملی گالیں گانیاں سیاں

میں بھجیا
کونجے ڈاری ماری سی
اڈرھی سی جوڑ بنائ تے
سنبھلے نا پھل آیا سی
چیٹا جوڑا لائ تے

ایملی بیکڑے کھادی سی
بیڑا پیڑ اتکنا رہیا
نسوڑھے اتھروں سٹے سے
پلاں ماڑی اکھیں جمیاں

میں بئ گیاں بٹ ٹشنا لائ تے
تارے ماڑی انکھیں تروٹے
کہا اپر تریل پئ گئ

سنیتھا کھلتا تکنا سی
گنڈیرا اتھروں سٹناریا
چیڑاں واز بھجی سی

بنے نال روڑھے سے
ھتکورے مارے کسے بوجھے

کمیلے میلی اچھی ٹھالیا
چیلے کہار کھڑیا سی
دروے ھٹوں جانا ساں
پھواڑی کول فیر لوخ چھپی

بوڑ متاں دینی رئ
گولاں پیاں مسکنیاں سیاں
طوطے مور سوتے سے
آمبے ھٹ کو گو بولیا

کچی عمرے کنڈا چھپے
درد نکلے
لوخ پڑھے
لیت پھجے
اس سورنی کی محبت آخنے ن۔

I Had Gone to Search for a Poem

Hiding in the dark,
On a cold winter evening,
Before kuftan time.

The moon had not yet risen,
It was still early.
People were bringing their cattle in,
Chickens and goats could be heard.

Climbing onto the stonewall,
Jumping over thorny barriers,
Tangling with thons
I reached the top of the hill.

The city lights of Mirpur could be seen in the distance.
On the west side, the blinking lights of airplanes.

Guessing in the dark,
Searching in the night
Slipping in the mud
Getting lost in the fields
My eyes found that house
Where there stood the mulberry tree
That jhand grown in the yard wall
The unripen berry under the tree

I was tiny as a lime shoot
When the tip of the thorn pricked me
The woodchip stabbed me
I didn't know what they called this pain

Time kept passing,
I saw the berry ripen,
Watched its colour change.
I saw it turn yellow,
Entwining and coiling
like the blue vine

My hands longed to touch it,
To inhale its fragrance,
To seat it beside me.
But I hesitated,
Afraid it may respond with anger.
I thought to say, "I love you,"
But only in my heart.
What if she took off her slipper?

Time passed,
It grew late.
I watched the jhand turn red,
The berry ripen,
Her mirror pretending to scare the crows
Blinded me
Many a times
I pretended to frighten the parrots

Time kept moving,
I heard
The kunjal (amaltas) flowered
Dressed in a yellow.
The banana tree blossomed
The beauty of a swaheena

With the pride of a palm,
Roses sprayed it with perfume
The fragrance reached me,

I heard.
Toassi played the toalki
Romli sang the songs

I heard
The crane took flight
Becoming a pair, it flew
The flower of the semal tree arrived
Wearing white

Eamly was eaten by the baiker
The daft bhera watched
Nasoora shed tears
Crust gathered around my eyes

I sat leaning against a rock
Stars broke in my eyes
Dew fell upon the grass

The sanetha stood watching
The gandera continued to shed tears
The pines heard the sound
Stones had rolled with
my sobs reaching the stream

The kamila helped me up
The chilla took me home
I was going under the thruna tree

Near the phuwaar,
When the thorn pricked me again

The bhor offered advice
The gollaan stood smirking
The parrots and the peacocks were asleep
The owl spoke

When a thorn pricks in young age
Pain arises
The nib breaks in you
A chip tears you

That torment is called love

A loose translation of Sonnet 18 in Pahari-Pothwari

Awais Hussain

کے میں تگی اِک موسم بہار نے دیہاڑے نال ملاں

پر توں اُس تھیں وی زیادہ پیاری تے سوہنی ایں
تیز واہ نال بُور تے ٹالیاں شانکنیاں ن
تے گرمیاں نے دیہاڑے گھٹنے جانے ن
کائیں دفعہ دیں تھوں ڈاکی دُھپ نکڑنی اے
تے کائیں واری مٹھی وی اوئی جانی اے
قدرتی
پر توہاڑا سدا بہار کدے وی نی مکن لگا
نہ توہاڑی خوبصورتی کدے گھٹ اوئی سکنی اے
نہ موت وی تگی اپنے ساہے اندر لائی سکنی
کیاں جے توں اِس شاعری وچ ہمیشہ ہی جینی رہسیں

جچرانی بندے ساہ لہسن تے اکھیاں تگی سکسکن
اِچرانی اہ نظم وی جینی رہسی تے تگی زندہ رکھسی

Keh meiñ tuki ik mosam bihār ne diharey nāl milāñ

par tuñ us theeñ vi zedeh piyāri teh sohṇi eyñ
tez vāh nāl boor teh ṭaliyañ shānkniyañ
teh garmiyāñ ne diharey ghaṭney jāneyn
keiñ dafa deyñ thuñ ḍakmi dhup niklna
teh keiñ vāri maṭṭhi vi uwi jāni eh
teh har changi cheez ākhir par mukni eh
qadurti

par tuwāra sada bahār kadeh vi ni mukan-laghi
na tuwāri khubsūrti kadeh ghaṭ uwi sakni eh
na mōt vi tuki apne sāhey andar leyi sakni
kiyañ jey tuñ is shāri vich hamesha hi jeeni reyseyñ

jichrani bandey sāh lehsan teh akkhiyañ taki saksan
ichrani ey nazm vi jeeni reysi teh tuki zinda rakhsi

Sonnet 18
By William Shakespeare

Shall I compare thee to a summer's day?
Thou art more lovely and more temperate:
Rough winds do shake the darling buds of May,
And summer's lease hath all too short a date;
Sometime too hot the eye of heaven shines,
And often is his gold complexion dimm'd;
And every fair from fair sometime declines,
By chance or nature's changing course untrimm'd;
But thy eternal summer shall not fade,
Nor lose possession of that fair thou ow'st;
Nor shall death brag thou wander'st in his shade,
When in eternal lines to time thou grow'st:
  So long as men can breathe or eyes can see,
  So long lives this, and this gives life to thee.

Birmingham Grahn ni Shaadi

Nafeesa Hamid

Inspired by Afghan poetic form, Landays
(each couplet to have 22 syllables)

Oi oi, chaloh grahn ni shaadi meh shehrach das niya
Jaan Meh dasah tusahki suroh'a na grahn itha burmingam

Nazaak kuri ni shaadi utt oi, baleh baleh
Thusa soochya ohsi hava wich kuri boti banthi

Hai hai Chitta Kukar high-fi speaker pur, wah ji
Saariya gatiyah gatiyahn gaaliyah gaiyah

Hai soneh ni dhostalyah ai-yah
Lak-lak sohna lai tha sohniyah aiyahn

mureh acho kuriyah acho
prao: Benz, Audi, Porsche hire karo: Utt oi koreh tha kehrah

wah ji, Punjabi Hit Squad, pangra pao
sawel jiyah nacho, thup laghi Mughli mendhi-pur

hai kauri raath, hai akhri kaar, wah ji
dautri bunthi boti, havah-ch thakni patahkeh

Abu aandeh kebab samoseh, moor tha maarahn choroh
Ammi suji halweh naal mara muh mita kitha, jeev bandh

sitareh chankneh chankneh jaali neh picha
acho acho majwaanoh, mubarakah dyoh

maraaj doodh nee peena, lactose choohr
khala akhneh maraja-ki doodh baleh baleh dyoh

hai boleh chooriya, boleh kangna
wah ji amla lao kuriyoh, suweh tha sabz kapreh lao

Maasiyah handiyah bajoh bajoh
Ammi handi maroh! Shaadi bya aghleh shehr jiyah bolo

Pehno pehno ik toilet vich thyaariyah
prandeh fixers, eyelash gluers, cheela pinners wah

yeh kuriyah yeh kuriyah dil mariyah
the girls queue laughing, clapping, click clack clucking

hai hai dohl bajeh shahjeh mehmaan ai
wah ji chachi fighting khala over naan roti

huh maari kameez saadi suwi
hai shararah's and gararah's sabz safehd, Rani gold

sunoh: mereh yaar ki shaadi hai fir boloh
I didn't scowl oh how I, meh dandh kiya na dasah?

hai naani gaaliyah gaiyah dotri theh
choori chankana in grass, my lover heard me dance
hai mara dupatta thu luprya
my Irish bradari brought me bouquets of bangles

javaan mura, haseen kuri
my mazungu's name a beat in the heart of my palms

mulkaath banoh, maara kasoor kya?
my Kashmiri bradari brought my chola lengha

raath va sawel va, maariyahn chooriyah nach san
he pays a price to hear my bangles jangle by our bed

if pyaar hotha heh Sanam, who's Sanam? Asahn niya?
Hai hai and where do we go with loving from here mum?

Un meh changi nay lagthi? Thuki ka changa lagna jaanu
Was I too hard on you? On me, how fickle our love

pyaar hotha heh diwana sanam
then shall I die in your arms instead? Wah ji wah wah

Paveh maraaj Engrizi nach-o
paveh Panjabi tha paveh Multaani nach-o

Maa na roi, na roi rukhsati par maa
my brothers cried more than mum, don't cry yet mum not yet

hai sareh haseh paanj raatha thak
hai we laughed-cried five nights through maariyah mendhi nights

A Wedding at Home in Birmingham

Nafeesa Hamid

Oi oi, come on, let's go to the wedding at home, the city is lit up!
My love, tell me, did you bring the red for the wedding, or did you leave it in Birmingham?

The bride is dazzling—oh yes, oh yes!
Did you think she'd be floating in the air, a girl turned into a leaf?

Oh, the white rooster crows, the high-fi speakers' blast—wow!
Everywhere, old melodies mix with curses in song.

Oh, my beautiful friendships—ai-yah!
Thousands of beauties have gathered to celebrate.

My girls, my girls, come on!
Brothers, hire the Benz, Audi, Porsche—come on, let's roll!

Wow, Punjabi Hit Squad, let's get the bhangra going!
Dance all night, smear Mughlai mehndi on your hands.

Oh, what a grand night! Oh, the final ceremony—wow!
The bride, dressed like a doll, fireworks crackling in the wind.

Father arrives with kebabs and samosas, uncles snatch them away.
Mother, with semolina, halwa, sweetens everyone's mouths, ties hearts together.

The stars twinkle and sparkle behind the netted veil.
Come, come, dear guests, give your blessings.

The groom doesn't drink milk—he's lactose-intolerant!
Aunt laughs—"Give the groom the ceremonial milk anyway!"

Oh, the bangles jingle, the bracelets chime—wow!
Girls, bring the henna, tomorrow we wear green.

The aunties are in the kitchen, pots clanking.
"Mother, hit the pan! Let's talk about the next wedding in another city."

Sisters, squeeze into one bathroom to get ready.
Braid-fixers, eyelash-gluers, scarf-pinners—what a sight!

Oh, these girls, these girls, my heart melts!
They queue up, laughing, clapping, click-clack giggling.

Oh, the drums beat, the special guests arrive!
Wow—Aunty and Khala fighting over naan and roti.

Oh no! My dress got caught on a needle!
Oh, the shararas and gararas—green, white, rani gold.

Listen: it's my beloved's wedding—say it again!
I didn't frown, oh how could I? Did I not show my teeth in a smile?

Oh, Grandmother curses under her breath, her eyes teary.
My bangles clink on the grass—my beloved hears me dance.

Oh, my dupatta, it slipped away!
My Irish family brought me bouquets of bangles.

A young groom, a radiant bride,
My white beloved's name beats in the heart of my palms.

It was meant to be, what was my fault?
My Kashmiri family brought my embroidered lehenga.

The night passes, the dawn arrives, my bangles still dancing.
He pays a price to hear them jangle by our bed.

If love was madness, oh beloved, who is this madness for?
Oh, oh, and where do we go with this love, Mum?

Did you not like me then? What kind of love was this, my dear?
Was I too hard on you? On myself? How fickle love can be.

Love is meant to be wild, my beloved,
Then shall I die in your arms instead? Wow, oh wow.

Come on, dance in English style!
Come on, dance in Punjabi and Multani style!

Mother, don't cry—not yet, not at the farewell.
My brothers cried more than Mum—don't cry yet, Mum, not yet.

Oh, we laughed and cried for five long nights,
Oh, how we laughed through these mehndi nights.

Mey Pyaar Kitha Si

Nafisa Akhtar

Muhabatan kithaban vich ni sikhina
ay darvazay har dillan vich ni ohnay, una vich barray raaz
chappay veyn
Pyar karney aley chuniey jaanein

Mey bey hisaab pyaar kitha, had thu zyada
Muhabbath nal pura dil ditha
Maray buay teh darvazay, har jaga band san
Dillan niyaa kandaa barriyan uchiyan san
Keh pata dil luttan alay keyrey paasu ai san

Jisleh thu milya sey mari sari dunya badli gi si
Thari har sheh changi lagni si
Awaz thu maarein, teh mara dil jaagi pehna si
Akhiyan phullan nay haar satniya san
Pyaar miki anniya kitha
Jeyray swaal mey puchay, vapas thu soh jawaab dithey

Mein jo mangya, thu vapas zaar vaar ditha
Badami akhiyan thariyan, miki gulaaban ni baaghan
vich kehd kitha
Is kehdi vich mey barri khush azaad sa
Pyaar ney pinjray vich koi taalay chabiyan ni ohnay
Mey khirri gi sa, suni teh, thariyan laadliyan piyaar
niya ghallan

Un thari yaad achni, teh dil barra khush ohna
Thariyan ghallan yaad kithiyaa
Thara naa bulaya- thari har ghal satai
Thuki lohri lohri teh mey khoi gi ah
Ishq muhabath kari teh mey apne apey ki milli ah

Dil ni narmiyaan akhan thak pohnchi giyan
Otan ni beychehniyaan lafzan ki maari giyan
Kan maray koi awaaz ni sunnay
Keh patha, harre oh bulaye, teh dil jawab deysi
Keh kariyeh, oh din usne nal... ni pulnay
Mey bey hisaab pyaar kitha, had thu zyada
Vakaey muhabbath nal pura dil ditha

I loved once

Love is not to be learnt from books
Unique openings and mysteries not for every heart
Lovers are chosen

I loved once, beyond measure, wholeheartedly
The chambers of my heart and all its passages were closed
It's walls too tall to climb
Who knows, from where he came...the one who stole my heart?

The day I met you, my whole world turned upside down
I loved everything about you
Whenever you called my name, my heart came to life
As if your words were petals, showering me like confetti
Your love blinded me
Whatever I asked, you gave a million times

Your almond eyes imprisoned me in a garden of roses
joyful and free in captivity
In love's confinement there are no locks or keys
I blossomed in the serenade of your devotion

Now memories of you warms my heart
Remembering your sweet nothings
Calling your name, torments
In search of you, I lost myself
But by this love, I found myself

The hearts' softness reaches the eyes and escapes in tears
The longing of the lips silences every word

My ears will hear no sound
Other than the sound of your voice calling me, maybe then my heart would answer
What can I do? Those days with you, are unforgettable
I love once, beyond measure
It's true...I really did give my whole heart in love.

Short Stories

Lucy

By Abdul Raouf Qureshi

لوسی تریاں پشتیاں سالاں کدے نی سمندرے سوہنی جنانی سی ۔ میں اسکی ٹرین سٹیشنے اپروں چایا او ہوں تاولی سی کیڑے ویلے سکول پھجی تے اپنے منڈے کی چے میں اے غل تنویر کی بائ تنویر آخنا میکی دسو لوسی سوہنی تے ھے سی دسنی کیجی سی تنویر اپنی اکھ نوٹی خیالاں وچ پیا سوچن لگا لوسی کیجی دسنی ھوئ جھلے کوئ تھو پیر نیس لگا لاکھ ماریس آلا فیر لوسی کیجی دسنی سی میں تنویر نی غلے کی لپڑی اسنے انداز وچ تھوڑی وازے اوچی وچ آخیا جھلے میں اسکی پک اپ کیتا او صرف بے دسنی سی

استوں پہلے کے تنویر کوئ ہور بے ھودہ سوال کرے اسکی موقعہ دیتیاں بغیر میں غل روڑی ٹریفک زید سی لوسی کڑی کڑی ماڑے کولوں پچھے کتنی دیری وچ سکول پجساں میں اسکی دسیا ٹریفک سکول ٹیم زیدے ھوئ جانی اے دو چار منٹ ھٹ اپر ھوئ جاسن اس ماڑی اس نی غل بھجی ای نی سکولے کول پچھے تے او سڑکے نے دوھے پاسے میکی اے بائ ٹی گئ توں گڈی موڑی آن میں منڈے کی کینی گیڈے اپر ملساں میں واپس آیاں اسکی ٹیکسی وچ بھالیا اسنا منڈا زیدے خوش نی سی اسنے اکھیاں وچ اتھروں سن لوسی منڈے کولوں پوچھیا منہ کیاں بسو رنا ایں ۔ کوسے کچھ آخیا سے کچھ منڈا استاں سالاں ناسی ماؤ دلاسا دیتا او زور زور نال رونا بان لگا میکی کلاسے منڈے نال نی بہن دینے آخن سن سورے نا رام گوشت کھائ ساڑھے نال نہ بو۔

لوسی تھپی تے بولی میں اس سکولے کولوں اکی (تنگ) گیاں آں اس اپنے نال غل کیتی سی ماڑے کن کھیلی گے

میں ساری غل بھجی سی منڈے نے اتھروں ھن ھتکوریاں وچ بدلی گے سن ۔ لوسی اسکی دلاسہ دئ پلان لغی

میں ھیڈ ٹچر کی رپورٹ کرساں نال آخیاس اگلے سال میں توکی دوئے سکول داخل کراساں منڈا جسنا ناں آرچی سی مکس ریس دسنا سی نا موقعہ سی نا کوئ تک بننی سی کے میں لوسی کولوں پچھاں آرچی ناپیو

بنگالی اے پاکستانی یا کشمیری آرچی نانک نقشہ دسنا سی کے اسنا آپو انہاں ملخاں وچوں اے۔ ٹیکسی ڈرائیونگ کوئ سوخا کم نی بچیاں تھوں کنی بڈھیاں تکڑ سب جانے پینے ن۔ غل سوچی سمجھی منواں کڈنی پینی اے م شیشے وچوں پچھے تکیا لوسی ڈونگی سوچ پئی ماڑے داخ تکنی پئی سی م آپوں لاجم (شرمندہ) ساں نا ماڑا ذکرا سی نا ماڑے کول تسلی نے لفظ ناکوئ جئ تعلیم کے م سورے کی اس بچے تھیں حلال آخی سکاں۔

لوسی ماڑھی مشکل آسان کیتی او ھک پرفیشنل جنانی سی. پہلیں لوسی سکولے وچ بچیاں کی پڑانی رھئ بعد وچ او سوشل ورکر پھرتی ھوئ گی اسنی سکول نی جاب پرئمری نے بچیاں کی پڑھانا سی بچیاں کی واک اپ کھڑنا انہاں تھیں آرگنائز کرنا مسیتیاں مندراں چرچاں گردواریاں وچ وی اس بچیاں کی سیر کرائ سی

انہاں کی پادریاں مولویاں نال ملایا سمیس۔ کے بچے سکھی جان سارے مذاہب دوئے نی عزت کرنے

انہاں نے مذھب نا احترام کرنے امن پیار محبت سلوک اتفاق سے رھنے نی تعلیم دینن۔

لوسی صرف سوھنی ای نی سی اسکی غل کرنے ناچج (سلیقہ) وی سی اسنی غلاں تھوں پتا لگا اسنے ماپیو آئرلینڈ تھوں انگلینڈ آئے سن لوسی نی پیدائش مانچسڑ ھوئ مانچسڑ وچ دنیا نے ھر ملک مذھب نسل نے لوک بسنے ن

ملٹی کلچر سوسائٹی وچ رھی ھورناں ملخاں نے کڑیاں منڈیاں نال پڑھی بہنے نال لوسی بھوں کجھ سنیا

میں حیران ھویا جیلے لوسی میکی اسلام نے بارے وچ دسن لگی۔ میں پچھے سویئر (بغیر) نہ رھی سکیا توں

اتنا کجھ کھتوں پڑھیا۔ تنویر جیڑا اجے تکڑ لوسی نے ٹوٹے جوڑناپیا سی میکی آخنا بے مقصد ایئ جی جنانی نی پھسنی

میں تنویر نی مشکل آسان کیتی ماڑی گوڈ لک لوسی آخیا میکی اولڈ ٹریفرڈ ڈیکھنی چل آرچی اسنی چولی وچ سر رکھی ستا وا پاسے ماری جے گرمی چنگی پلی سی لوسی آرچی نا سر سیدھا کیتا اپنی قمیصے نے بیڑے کھولیس پرسینا اسنی چھاتیاں اپر پانیئے اروڑنا جے تنویر ماڑے داخ تکن لگا تنویر بچھنا چاہنا سی ہور کہ تکیا او لوسی نی گول چھاتیاں نا نقشہ بنای تکنا چاہنا سی لوسی کتنی سوہنی ہوئ ہوسی۔ وزن اپنے مونڈیاں نال بنی ٹرنی پھرنی کیچی دسنی ہوئ ہوسی۔

لوسی آرچی داخ تکی دسیا دسیا پیو اسنا پیو مسلمان اے ساجد نال ماڑی ملاقات کالج وچ ہوئ سی ساجد چنگا کپی مندا سی تھوڑے ٹیمے وچ ساڑی جان پشان دوستی وچ بدلی گی۔ ہک دہہ باڑے ساجد مذاق کیتی لوسی چیلے میں تکی تکنا آن شطان میکی ککٹاریاں کڈنا اے۔ ساجد کوئ کٹر (سٹرکٹ) قسم نا مسلمان نی سی کہ ٹوپی لائ تسبیح چائ دسنا پھیرنا رے۔ اسکی اتنا احساس جے سی کے کدرے ساڑھے بشکار لائن ہیئے جسکی پار نی کرنا چاہی نا

لوسی دسیا میں تے کدھے شطان نی سی تکیا لا پیو کرسیجن سن چیلے میں نکی ساں او میکی چرچ کھڑنے رے فیر انہاں نی آخیا اچھ ساڑھے نال جل۔

فیر جدوں وی گئ اپنی مرضی نال ساجد نال ماڑا رشتہ کوئ را توُ رات نی سی بنیا اساں دو سال کالج وچ گھٹیاں گزارے سن ہک سال یونیورسٹی وچ اساں ہک دوئے کی پسند کرنے ساں ماڑا کہار مانچسٹر شہرے وچ سی

یونیورسٹی ٹورنے پنڈسے اپر فیر وی میں (چوز) کیتا اپنی تعلیم کہار تھوں بار رہی میکی مکمل کرساں ماڑھے ماء پیو خوش سن کے میکی انڈپینڈنٹ زندگی گزارنے نا تجربہ ہوسی۔ نال میں یونیورسٹی نی زندگی کی چنگی

- 152 -

ترے انجوائے کرساں میں اپنے کہارے تھوں چار پنج میل دور ہک سہیلی نال رہن پئی۔ ساجد اسے علاقے وچ فلیٹ شیئر کرنا سی۔ وقت گزرنے نال اساں زیدے ہوئے (کلوز) ہوئے گے اساں گھٹے کلباں وچ جانے ساں

ساجد شراب نی سی پینا میں کدھے کدھرے چسکی لانی ساں۔

اساں کی لاک ڈاون ٹریفک وچ پھسیاں کافی دیر ہوئی گیا۔ لوسی اسنے بارے کوئی غل نی کیتی لوسی پورے اطمنان نال میکی ساجد نال گزرے وقت نی کہانی سنانی رہی اساں جن وچ کافی بے تکلفی ہوئی گی سی۔

میں لوسی نال زیدے ماحول کمفی وچ غل کرنے تھیں شیشہ اسرے سیٹ کیتا جیتھے میں لوسی نال غلاں کرنیاں اسکی چنگی ترے تکی سکاں۔ تنویر لوسی نیاں چھاتیاں ناں حساب جوڑی بتی سی نی ضرب دیتی فیر ہلکے گلابی رنگے نی برا وچ بنی لوسی نے دس سائز نے لکے نال بدھا۔ اے اگست نی غل اے۔ اس دہیاڑے چنگی تپالی پئنی پئی سی۔ لوسی نا گورا رنگ چمکنا گلابی دسے اس اپنے بلونڈ بال انگلیاں نی کنگی وچ سیدھا کرنیاں غل ٹوری رکھی یونیورسٹی نے دوئے سال میں تے ساجد فلیٹ شئر کری کیندا

اساں کی ہک دوئے نی عادت ہوئی گی کہار ہتھ لپڑی ہک دوہے کی تکنے راں آپے کی اکھیاں اولے نہ ساں ہون دینے ہک دوئے نیاں ضرورتاں نا خیال وی رکھنے ساں۔ ہک دہیاڑے میکی کپڑے آئے وسئے سے

میں زیدے تکلیف وچ ساں جسمانی ضرورتاں ناپورا ہونے تھوں کمپلیکیشن ڈیولپ ہوئی ری سی۔ مارا دل کرے کوئی مارا خیال کرنے آلا وے ساجد میکی گرم پانئے نی بوتل دتی میں ساجد نا ہتھ لپڑی کول بالی کیندا

اسنے منویں کی تلیاں نی کولی وچ رکھی تکن پئی ساجد ماڑہے بالاں نے انگلی اپر چھلے بنانا میکی دلاسے دین

لغا

ساجد ماڑھے روا ٹھیاں کی ہتھ لے کدے انگلی نال ہوٹاں کی چھیڑے اساں گھنٹیاں نے ساوھک دوئے کی تکنے رئے ہوساں ساجد ادھا جیا لیٹیا ماڑی چھاتیاں اپر سر رکھی سئ گیا۔

تنویر جلدی جلدی لوسی نی ہاف سلیو لغیاں باہناں اپر دعا ار اٹھے ہتاں تا نقشہ بنایا لوسی نی کڑیاں واں باں

گورے ہتاں نیاں لمیاں انگلیاں نے چٹے نوں بھوں سوہنے دسن لوسی دسن لغنی دوہے دہہاڑے مڑا وجود ہلوا ہوئ گیا جسم نی پھوک زیدے بدھی گی موسم چنگا سی ساجد میکی بلیک پول سمندر کنارے کنی گیا۔

لہنا دھیں چڑھنا چن ترکڑی اپر سن اس دیہاڑے اساں بچے بنی گے ساجد تبعن شرمیلا سی اس دیہاڑے اسکی کوئ پروانی سی اساں کھیڑنے سپیہاں چننے ریتے اپر پھل بوٹے بنانے ہک دھوئے نے نا لنکھے ہتھ لڑی سمندرے وچ جائ کھلتے ساڑھے نک متتے ہوٹ ہک ہوئ گے اساں نا جوغے ای کپڑے لائے وے سن

سمندرے نا پانی ساڑے ننگے جسیاں کی چوٹے دین لغا ساجدنیاں انگلیاں ماڑھے گھاٹے نی زنجیری نے تیوں نال کیہڑن پیاں فیر اساں جھمی ماری کیندی ساڑھے ہتھ کنڈاں تھوکنے بندڑیاں اپر جائ کھلتے سمندرے نے کھارے پانئے ترے ہور بدھائ تنویر موقعے نی تلاش وچ سی اس لوسی نے پٹاں تھوں پیراں تکٹر

ویکس ہویاں چمکنیاں لتاں نا سکیچ بنایا ۔ لوسی نی پینیاں اوتلے پانیاں وچ مچھیاں ارپڑکنیاں دسن گورے گودلے پیر پائلے نال بھجے چانی وچ تہوتے دسے۔

لوسی ساجد نال گزرے وقت نی کہانی آرچی نے بالاں اپر ہتھ پھیر نی ساجد نی خشبو سیکھنی ڈونگے پانیاں وچ ڈوبی جے لوسی دسن لغی کھجاں دھیاڑیاں بعد میں ٹھیک ہوئی گی اس دھیڑے میں گلابی قمیض سبز شلوار نال میچنگ چیلہ رکھیا ماڑی بہاں وچ کچے نیاں بنگاں سن اے خاص تحفے جیڑے ساجد ماڑھے تھیں میرپوروں آندے سن میں سانبھی رکھے وے سے کشمیری بوٹیاں بہوں سوہنیاں ہونیاں ن اس راتیں اے خاص ساجد تھیں تیار ہوئی میں کناں وچ مندریاں بیاں نکے وچ کوکا لوسی نے نشیلے رسیلے رنگیلے ہوٹاں کی میک اپ نی لوڑ نی سی اسنے کتابی منوہیں اپر چمکنی بلوریں اکھیاں نے پمیلاں نا ہک بال تروٹانی سی دسنا

پھر مٹے ستے کمانے وچ تنی تیرے ار اس راتیں لوسی اپنے چمکنے متھے اپر بندی ساجد نے نانی لائی نہ ٹہول ٹمپکے ہوئے نہ کوسے سیرا گانا بدھا لوسی دسیا ساڑھے دلاں ملنے نے گیت گائے ساڑھی روحاں انہاں اپر رقص کیتا

ساڑھے ہوٹاں سمی ہائی سی ۔

اس راتیں میں چنبے نی بیل بنی ساجد نال پلپیچی ساجد نے ساں نال پھل کھڑے ساجد اپنے ہوٹاں نال ماڑھے جسے اپروں خشبو چنتی اساں کپڑے بٹائے اساں اپنے نواں نال نگے پنڈیاں اپر نالنی ساری زندگی ھک دوھے نال رہنے نیاں قسماں کھادیاں میں گھونگٹ کڈی نہ ساں بھئی ہتاں نی پھٹے اپر ٹھوڈی رکھی ماڑی اکھیاں ساجد نی راہ ڈیکی ماڑھے تہک تہک کرنے دلے ساجد نا سہرا گایا سی ساجد نے ہوٹاں ماڑھے ہتاں اپر مہندی لائی

ماڑے ار ساجد وی بہوں خوش سی اومچی مچی پائلاں بھجے اساں کی دنیا جانے نی ہوش نہ رہی اس راتیں ماڑی بنگ پچی ساڑھے گاٹیاں نے رتے لال نشاں ساڑے رشتے نے گواہ بنے میں سویلے ساجد نا ہتھ لپڑی اپنے کہار امی ابے نال شامیں ڈنر اساں ساجد نے کہار اسنے امی ابے نال کیتا ۔

اتنا دسی میں تنویر نے منویں داخ تکیا اُو لوسی نے پانہے اربیٹھے نیڑھے اپر ہتھ پھیر نا لوسی نی تنی نا چھلہ سیدھا کرن لغا جیسنے وچ ناری رنگے ناتیوا چمکنا دسیاس پلَے ویلے کی یاد کرنی لوسی نی واز بَجھن لغی اس چلنی کارے نا شیشہ بہنے کیتا آرچی کی چائے لپنی چھاتی نال چھوڑیا اسنا حال ڈری وی پیڈے آلا سی جسنا دودھ پنیا بچہ گیڈرے چائے کھڑیا وے ادھ کھلے شیشے وچوں سمانے داخ چڑاں وچ ترونٹے چَنَے کی تکلی لوسی دسیا شادی نے پہلے دو سال بھوں چنگے گزرے ساجد میکی پھولاں ار رکھیا میں خشبو ہنی اسنے نال اُڈرنی رہی اساں گھٹیاں چرچاں وی گے مسیتاں وچ وی سارٹھے اپر مذہب نا رنگ چڑھن پیا ساجد جمعہ نی سی کھنجنا میں ہر تاریں چرچ جانی ساں۔

آرچی جیچرے ہلک سالے نا ہونا ساجد چنگا پلا مسلمان ہوئی گیا اوپچ ٹیم مسیتی جان پیا داڑھی رکھی کیندی

بال بدھائ چھنڈ وی للے بالاں نے چھتے اسکی چنگے سوہنے سن۔ آرچی دو سالاں نانی سی چیلے ساجد دوستاں نال کشمیر گیا۔ چیلے مڑیا اسنے رنگے بدلے وے اُو میکی شادی نا آخن لغا میں لپنی خوشی نال جائی ٹاون حال وچ شادی رجسٹری نی تاریخ کیندی اچھی ساجد کی سرپرائز دیتا ساجدنی منیا اُو زوردین لغا میں کلمہ پڑھی اسنے نال نکاح کراں میکی اے غل نی سی منظور مذہب بندے کی چنگا انسان تکنا چاہنا اے۔

نکاح ووز (vows) مندرے وچ پھیرے مذھبی رسماں ن کے لوکوں کی پتا لگے کڑی منڈا ہلک ہوئی گے ن۔ ولیمہ پارٹیاں وی سیم تِنگ (same thing) ن خاندان دوستاں وچ شادی نا اعلان کرنا مقصد ہونا اے۔ میں ساجد اپر بیوی ہنی محبتاں نجاور کیتیاں اکھ چائے کوسے غیر مرد کی نی تکیا نہ بے وفائی کیتی سارا جیڑا وقت گٹھا گزریا ساجد اس تعلق کی میاں بیوی نا رشتہ منّے تیار نی سی ساجد کول اس سوال نا جواب وی نی سی اُو کیڑے رشتے نال ماڑھے نال سینا رہیا۔ سباں کی پتا سی اساں میاں بیوی

آں۔ ساڑا منڈا اے۔ دو سالاں تھوں گھٹے رہنے پئے آں۔ اساں ھک دوئے کی چنگا پرکھی رشتہ بنایا سی۔ ساجد آرچی کی نا جائز اولاد آخی ماڑی محبت نی توھین کیتی۔

اس دھیڑے پہلی واریں ماڑا میڑ پھریا میں ساجد کی آخیا دفعہ ھوئ جا لوسی نی غل بجھی جسرے میکی چپ لگی سی تنویر و دی اے ترے چویتا برش لپڑی رنگ رکھی کھلی گیا او تصویر مکمل کرنا چاھنا سی تنویر روح نی سی بائ سکنا باقی اس کوئی قمر نی چھوڑی لوسی ناک منہ چپئے دند دھوتے اپر تل موندیاں ٹکڑ بال ناک مہتہ بالکل لوسی اردیسے۔

تنویر لوسی نی سلو اربنان لگا فیر برش رکھی ماڑھے داخ تکیاس پہلیں میں کہانی پوری کراں فیر او تصویر وچ رنگ پرے میں غل ٹوری رکھی نہ چاھنے نے باوجود میں لوسی کولوں پوچھیا کہ تساں نال رشتہ فیر ختم ھوئ گیا

ساجد کہروں گیا لوسی اٹھی نے منویں اپر پیار دھی دسیانی رشتہ ھور پکا ھوئ گیا دوئے دھیڑے ساجد کہار مڑی آیا چھ مینے گزری ھور بیوی بنی اسنی خدمت کرنی ری اے حق سمجھی اپنی ھوس پوری کرنا رھیا۔ ماڑا ساجد سوھنیاں سوھنیاں مہنگیاں پرفیوماں نا عاشق سی او عطر فروشاں نے ھتھ چڑی گیا

پکڑی جے سیور اسناد ین مکمل نی سی ھونا جمعہ مبارک نے میسج عطر لوانا جمعراتیں نا لنگر۔ بس اتنی اسنی سوشل لائف رہی گی۔

ساجد محفلاں نی جان ھونا سی جیا برین واش ھویا ھور ناں مسلک فرقیاں نے لوکاں کی کافر سمجھی انہاں نے ایمان کی شک نال تکن لگا۔ میں ساجد نے انہاں کرتوتاں کولوں تنگ بسیوا کرنی ری چھ مہنیاں بعد

آرچی ترے سالاں نا ہوئی گیا ھک دھیڑے میں کے اپروں آئی تکیا ساجد آرچی نی باں نال ساوی ٹاکی بدھی وی نعرے جلیاں مارے پیا میں پڑھی لکھی جنانی آں۔ٹی وی تکنی آں خوراں (خبراں) بھجنی آں کے اپر ماڑا واہیت پیتے نے لوکاں نال پینا اے۔

دنیا نے حالاات کی میں جاننی آں۔ مذھب مسلک فرقے سیاست قوم نسل برادری وچ بندی پہلیں لوکاں نی ذھن سازی کیتی جانی اے فیر ضرورت ویلے انہاں کی استعمال۔ میکی آخیاں افسوس ہونا اے اے سب ھر ملخے مذھب وچ اے ترے سالاں نا دودھ پینا کڑی منڈا جسنے سیدے پیر نہ پینے وین اسنے سامنے نچنا not acceptable to me بچہ جس مرضی ملخے مذھب نا وے۔ کچی عمرے نیاں تکیاں بھجیاں وقت گزرنے نال پکیاں ہوئی جانیاں ن دنیا وچ سب تھوں زیدے قتل مذھب نے نا اپر ہونا ن۔ انتہا پسند لوکاں کی ورغلائی مذھب نے ناں اپر انہاں نے بچے کوانے ن۔ او ماڑے تھیں فیصلے نی کڑی سی اتھے ساجدنی جنے جوزف ھونا تاں وی میں ایئے کراں اریم ساجد اپر کہار نے دروازے بند کری آخیا ھن کدے ادھر مڑی نہ نکیں۔

کراسنگ اپر کھلتیاں سیٹیاں بجانی ریلے نی وازے وچ ڈوبی لوسی اپنی غل توڑ چاڑی میں کگڑی نہ جسنے بچے نول چائ کرسن نہ بکری آں کی ماڑھے بچے قصائ کونے تھیں کنی جان۔ میں ما آں۔ میں آرچی کی پڑھائ چنگا نسان بناساں۔ کدھے درندہ نہ بنن دین لگی۔ لوسی نا سٹاپ آئ گیا سی میں پچھیا ساجد ھن کتھے اے لوسی دسیا
حوراں نے لشکارے نی سنس چلن ھوئے سالے بعد ھک واری معافی منگنے تھیں۔ میں منہ نی لایا۔
ماڑی غل توڑ چڑی تنویر رنگ برش چائ کندے تنویر صرف مصور نی سی اسکی تصویر وچ جذبات نے

رنگ پرنے وی اچھنے سن اس لوسی نی تتی بنایا الڑہ بنایا تھلے الڑے انٹیاں وچ بلبل بھالیس اپر بلبل بھالیس فیر ھک سپ لوسی نی پھنی نال پلیچیا گوٹھے تکڑ پھجنا جسنا کھلا منہ انٹیاں کی تاڑنا سی۔

Lucy

Lucy was a beautiful woman of medium height, around thirty-five years old. When I picked her up from the railway station, she was in a hurry, concerned about reaching school on time to pick up her son.

When I told Tanveer about this, he asked, "Tell me, was Lucy beautiful, what did she look like?" Tanveer, closed his eyes, was lost in thought, trying to imagine what Lucy looked like.

When he couldn't picture her in his mind, he winked and asked again, "Tell me, how beautiful was she?"

Understanding Tanveer's curiosity, I replied in a slightly louder voice, imitating his style, "When she sat in my car, she looked like a mother."

Before Tanveer could ask any other inappropriate questions, I continued, not giving him a chance to speak.

The traffic was heavy, and Lucy kept asking how much longer it would take to reach the school. I told her that the traffic increases around school times, so it would be a few minutes' delay.

It felt like she hadn't even heard me. When we reached near the school, she got out on the other side of the road, saying, "You turn the car around and meet me at the school gate with my son."

I drove back and picked her up again. Her son wasn't very happy; there were tears in his eyes. Lucy asked him, "Why are you making that face? Did someone say something?"

The boy, around seven or eight years old, started crying loudly when his mother asked. He explained, "The other boys in the class won't let me sit with them. They say I shouldn't sit with them because I eat pork."

Lucy, angry, said, "I'm fed up with the atmosphere at this school."

She had spoken to herself, but I heard everything. The boy's crying turned into sobs. Lucy comforted him and said, "I will complain to the headmaster. And next year, I'll get you enrolled in another school."

The boy, whose name was Archie, looked like he was of mixed race. There was no opportunity or reason for me to ask Lucy if Archie's father was Bengali, Pakistani, or Kashmiri. From Archie's appearance, it seemed his father belonged to one of those countries.

Driving a taxi is not an easy job. It's about picking up everyone, from children to the elderly.

You need to think carefully before speaking. I looked at Lucy through the rearview mirror, she was lost in deep thought, gazing at me. I felt ashamed. I had neither the courage nor the right words to comfort her, and I certainly had no religious knowledge to tell her that pork was permissible for the boy.

Lucy made it easier for me. She was a professional lady. Initially, Lucy taught children at a school, and later she became a social worker. While working at the school, she not only taught primary school children but also took them on educational and field trips. She took them to mosques, temples, churches, gurdwaras, and other religious sacred places.

She introduced the children to religious leaders, so they could learn that all religions teach respect for one another and that people of different faiths should live in peace and harmony.

Lucy was not just beautiful; she had a way with words. From her conversation, I learned that her parents had come to England from Ireland. Lucy was born in Manchester, a city where people from every country, religion, and race live. Growing up in a multicultural society and studying with boys and girls from other countries, Lucy had learned a lot.

I was surprised when Lucy started explaining Islamic teachings to me. I couldn't help but ask her, "Where did you learn all of this?"

Tanveer, who had been imagining Lucy's figure in his mind, jokingly said, "A woman like that can't be trapped."

I made it easier for Tanveer, replying, "My good fortune!"

Lucy had told me to take her to Old Trafford. Archie, with his head resting on her lap, was sleeping, occasionally shifting his position. It was very hot. After adjusting Archie's head, Lucy unbuttoned her shirt. Sweat was flowing down her chest like water. Tanveer looked at me, clearly curious about what more I had seen. He seemed eager to know how Lucy looked, imagining the shape of her breasts and how it must have appeared while she was walking with the weight on her shoulders.

Lucy looked at Archie and told me that his father was Muslim. "I met Sajid at college," she continued. "Sajid was a very sociable guy. We became friends in no time. One day, jokingly, he said, 'Whenever I look at you, the devil tickles me.'"

Sajid was not a very devout Muslim who wore a cap or held prayer beads in his hand. He understood that there was a line between us that shouldn't be crossed.

Lucy explained that she had never seen the devil. Her parents were Christian, and when she was little, they used to take her to church. Later, they stopped asking her to join them. From then on, she went to church on her own whenever she felt like it.

"My relationship with Sajid didn't develop in a single night. We spent two years together at college and one year at university. We liked each other. My house was in Manchester city, within walking distance of the university. Despite this, I chose to live away from home and complete my studies. My parents were happy because they felt I would experience independence and enjoy university life."

I had been living about four to five miles away from home with a friend. Sajid was sharing a flat in the same area. Over time, we became quite close to each other. We used to go to clubs together. Sajid didn't drink alcohol; I would occasionally have a little. We had been stuck in traffic for quite a while due to the lockdown, but Lucy didn't mention it. Lucy calmly continued narrating stories about the time spent with Sajid. By now, we had become quite informal with each other. To converse comfortably with Lucy, I adjusted the mirror so I could see her clearly while we talked.

Tanveer worked out lucy's chest size "Then, tying the 32 inch light pink bra, he wrapped it around her size 10 waist. It was the month of August, there was a lot of sunshine that day. Lucy's fair skin was glowing in the sun, giving off a pinkish hue. She continued talking while straightening her blonde hair with her fingers. We were in our second year at university, and Sajid and I had shared a flat. We had gotten used to each other. At home, we would hold hands and gaze at each other for hours. We didn't let ourselves disappear from each other's sight. We took care of each other's needs.

One day, I wasn't feeling well. It was the time of my period. Due to unfulfilled physical needs, complication developed. I wished someone cared for me. Sajid brought a hot water bottle and gave it to me. I took Sajid's hand and made him sit next to me. I held his face in the palms of my hands and started looking at him. Sajid began playing with my hair, trying to comfort me. He touched my cheeks, sometimes teasing my lips with his fingers. That night, we spent a long time looking at each other. Sajid lay half-reclined and fell asleep. His head was on my chest. Tanveer quickly sketched the design of Lucy's half-sleeve arms. It seemed as Lucy's hands were raised in prayer. Lucy's toned arms and the long fingers of her fair hands with white nails looked very beautiful.

Lucy told me the next day she was feeling much better. Her desires were intensifying. The weather was nice. Sajid took her to Blackpool by the sea. The setting sun and the rising moon were on the scales. That evening, we became like children. Sajid's nature was shy, but that day, he didn't care about anyone. We played, picked seashells, made flower patterns on the sand, wrote each other's names, and holding hands, we stood in the sea. Our noses, foreheads, and lips became one. We were only wearing clothes in name. The blue water of the sea started to rock our bare bodies.

Sajid's fingers played with the gemstones in the necklace around my neck.
Our arms wrapped around each other's waists. Hands played with bodies, reaching the hips. The salty sea water intensified our desires.

Tanveer was looking for an opportunity. He created a sketch, from her thighs to her waxed and shiny legs. Lucy's feet were fluttering in the water like fish. The anklet around her fair chubby feet shone in the moonlight. Lucy shared stories of the time spent with Sajid, stroking Archie's hair, smelling Sajid's fragrance, immersed in his deep love. Lucy told me that after a few days, she was fine.

That day, I wore a pink kameez with green shalwar, and a matching green dupatta. My arms were adorned with glass bangles. These special gifts were brought by Sajid from Mirpur, which I had kept safe. Kashmiri brides are very beautiful.
That night, I had specially prepared for Sajid. I wore earrings, a nose ring,
and Lucy's dark, juicy, colourful lips needed no makeup. Not a single eyelash was broken on her face, which was like a book. Her eyebrows were curves like an archer's bow, with an arrow ready in it.

That night, Lucy placed a bindi on her shining forehead with Sajid's name on it.
There was no drum playing, nor was anyone singing a wedding song.

Lucy said that our hearts sang songs of union, and our souls danced to them.

Our lips sealed those moments. That night, I became a jasmine vine, wrapping around Sajid. Sajid's breath caused flowers to bloom. Sajid picked the fragrance of my body with his lips. We changed clothes, and on our bare bodies, with our nails, we wrote each other's names, making vows to stay together for a lifetime.
I did not sit with my veil lifted. With my chin resting on the back of my hands, my eyes waited for Sajid's return. My heart, racing, sang Sajid's praises.

Sajid's lips applied henna to my hands. Like me, Sajid was very happy.
He danced in joy like a peacock, swaying. We were oblivious to the world.
That night, my bangle broke. The red marks forming on our necks became witnesses to our relationship.

I took Sajid's hand the next morning and went to meet my parents. We had dinner at Sajid's house with his parents in the evening.
After sharing this, I looked at Tanveer. He was creating Lucy's smooth, flat tummy, his hand moving on her stomach, making a circle around her navel. In the centre of her belly ring, a red gem gleamed.

Lucy began to speak, reminiscing about the good times.

She lowered the window of the moving car, settled Archie against her chest.
Her condition was like a frightened sheep, whose baby had been taken by a wolf.

Through the half-open window, looking at the sky and the moon breaking through the clouds, Lucy said, the first two years of marriage were very good. Sajid treated me like I was on a bed of flowers. I flew with him like a fragrance. We went together to churches and mosques too.

We started embracing religion. Sajid regularly attended Friday prayers,
and I went to church every Sunday. By the time Archie turned one, Sajid had become a good Muslim. He prayed

five times a day and had grown a beard. His long hair flowing down to his shoulders. The long hair suited him well. When Archie was two, Sajid went to Kashmir with his friends. When he returned, his ways had changed. He wanted to marry me.

I agreed to marry him, so I went to the town hall to register our marriage. When I returned home, I shared the good news with Sajid. Sajid disagreed, insisting that I read the Kalma and marry him. I did not accept this. Religion wants to see a person as a good human. Nikah, vows, and the rituals around temples and gurdwaras are to announce the bond publicly. The purpose of walima parties and feasts is to make the marriage known to family and friends.

I showered Sajid with love as a wife, never once looking at another man. Nor was I ever unfaithful. The time we spent together, Sajid was not ready to accept it as a husband-wife relationship. Sajid had no answer to the question of what relation we had while living together all this time. Everyone knew we were husband and wife. We had a son together. We had been living together for two years, getting to know each other well. Sajid insulted my love by calling Archie an illegitimate child. That day, for the first time, I lost my temper. I told Sajid to leave.

After hearing Lucy's words, I became silent. Tanveer also stood silently, holding his brush, ready to continue painting. Tanveer could not add a soul to the picture, but he left no detail incomplete. Lucy's nose, face, white teeth, a mole on her lips, shoulder-length hair, were exactly like Lucy.

Tanveer started dressing Lucy in a shalwar. Then he put down the brush and looked at me, asking what next? Then he would fill the colours into the picture.

I continued with my words. Despite not wanting to, I asked Lucy, "So, did your relationship end?" Sajid left the house. Lucy, kissing Archie's face, replied, "No, the relationship became even stronger. The next day, Sajid returned home. Six months went by. I continued serving him as his wife. He continued to satisfy his desires, thinking it was his right."
My Sajid was fond of beautiful fragrant perfumes. He had fallen under the spell of perfume sellers. Now, without wearing a pagri or a cap, his religion didn't feel complete. "Jumma Mubarak" messages, making others wear perfume, Thursday's Langar (communal meal)—this was all that remained of his social life. Sajid was the life of gatherings, brainwashed to the point that he started viewing people from other sects as non-believers, questioning their faith. I kept enduring Sajid's beliefs.

Six months later, Archie turned three. One day, I returned from work and saw Sajid having tied a green cloth around Archie's arm and was making gestures. I am an educated woman. I listen to the news. I watch social media. At work, I interact with people of different kinds. I am well aware of the world's conditions. Religions, sects, politics, nationalism, race, and community condition people's minds first. Then, when needed, they are used. It pains me to say this, but this happens in every country and religion.

A three-year-old child, still drinking milk, who hasn't learned to walk properly yet. Dancing and parading in front of him is not acceptable to me.
A child, regardless of their country or religion, what they see at a young age, becomes ingrained in them. The most killings in the world happen in the name of religion. Extremists manipulate and incite people to kill their own children in the name of religion.

This was the moment of decision for me. If it had been a Joseph in front of me instead of Sajid, I would have done the same. I shut the doors of the house on Sajid and told him not to dare come back.

We were standing at the crossing. The sound of the passing train's whistles filled the air as Lucy continued speaking. "I am not a chicken whose chicks can be taken away. Nor am I a goat whose children can be slaughtered by the butcher, and I will just watch. I am a mother, and I will educate Archie to become a good human being.
I will never let him become a beast."

It was Lucy's stop.

I asked, "Where is Sajid now?"

Lucy replied, "The allure of the heavenly houris didn't suit him. He returned after a year to ask for forgiveness. I didn't acknowledge him."

My words were finished, and Tanveer picked up his brush and painted. Tanveer was no ordinary artist; in his paintings, the colours of emotions were visible too. He created a nest beneath Lucy's bellybutton, and in the nest, a bulbul was chirping on eggs. Then, a snake wrapped around Lucy's calf, reaching up to her knee, its open mouth gazing at the eggs with a tempting look.

This story was translated and edited by Abdul Raouf Qureshi and Nabeela Ahmed